WHO GOES HOME?

books by SYLVIA WAUGH

The Ormingat Trilogy

Space Race
Earthborn
Who Goes Home?

WHO GOES HOME?

Sylvia Waugh

Delacorte Press

Published by
Delacorte Press
an imprint of
Random House Children's Books
a division of Random House, Inc.
New York

Text copyright © 2003 by Sylvia Waugh
Jacket illustration copyright © by Martin Matje

Originally published in Great Britain in 2003 by The Bodley Head,
an imprint of Random House Children's Books

Visit us on the Web! www.randomhouse.com/kids
Educators and librarians, for a variety of teaching tools, visit us at
www.randomhouse.com/teachers

Library of Congress Cataloging-in-Publication Data
Waugh, Sylvia.
Who goes home? / Sylvia Waugh.
p. cm.
Summary: On his thirteenth birthday, Jacob learns a secret about his birth and
becomes involved in his father's work to protect other beings from the planet
Ormingat who live on Earth.
ISBN 0-385-72965-0—ISBN 0-385-90160-7 (lib. bdg.)
[1. Extraterrestrial beings—Fiction. 2. Fathers and sons—Fiction. 3. England—
Fiction. 4. Science fiction.] I. Title.
PZ7.W35115Wh 2004
[Fic]—dc21
2003048451

The text of this book is set in 11.1-point Joanna MT.

Book design by Kenny Holcomb

Printed in the United States of America

April 2004

10 9 8 7 6 5 4 3 2 1
BVG

For
Gary and Ruth Porteous

And in loving memory of my brother-in-law,
Brian Porteous

CONTENTS

We are all souls in the same small universe.

Earthborn

The Naming

Infringement! Infringement! Rules are clear. Rules are meant for your protection, Sterekanda.

Steven looked innocently up at the green cube, which flickered as sound waves passed beneath its glassy surface. The spaceship, where he now sat, was the same as always. Steven had paid frequent visits over the past three years and had carried out all instructions to the very letter.

So where was the infringement?

The infringement lay in his arms. A baby was snuggled up close to him, swaddled in a white silk shawl. It began to whimper.

"Hush," said Steven softly. "Hushaby."

Children of mixed parentage do exist. But they should never be presented. The communicator made its pronouncement flatly.

Steven let the baby grasp his forefinger. He looked down at the helpless, pale little face and stooped to kiss its broad brow. The grating voice of the machine was no lullaby for a sick child.

An Earth womb birthed this infant. He is Earthling.

"He is my son," said Steven firmly. "His mother is my wife."

Ormingatrig who unite with Earth ones are not approved.

"But allowed," said Steven quickly. "It is allowed. I have consulted the rules."

Only if unspoken.

"It was unspoken," said Steven, "till necessity drove me to this. Without our help, my son would have died."

Children die. Life loses infants on Earth. That is known.

"But infants are not lost on Ormingat," said Steven. "On Ormingat no child is lost."

He said this with conviction and the machine did not contradict him. The knowledge on which his statement was built was pure intuition. He had lived on Earth for three years, and was expected to live here for a further seventeen. As with all visitors from Ormingat, the peaceful planet, he had lost most of his memories of the place and of its language. These would be stored against his return, when his body would revert to being an Ormingat body, and his brain would be once more an Ormingat brain. On Earth he needed Earth memories and an earthly mother tongue. So he was an Englishman, living in London and working as a freelance computer expert, well respected for his talents and never lacking the normal Earth employment that covered his real reason for being here.

Steven was not primarily an observer, as others were. He was an arranger, a facilitator. Those he helped he would never meet. It was all down in the rule book: Ormingat workers on the planet Earth, whatever their function, should never connect. It was not part of their brief to make any change to the planet that was not within the capacity of ordinary human beings.

"I brought Jacob here that his life might be saved," said Steven. "Earth does not possess the medicine we need."

It is a misuse of power. You must know that.

Jacob had ceased to whimper and had fallen into a calm, sweet sleep. The mativil was working. The baby's tiny system was settling into comfort as the elixir Steven had fed him cruised gently round inside his body. Spaces were filled up. Gaps were repaired. In his sleep he still held tightly on to his father's finger.

Steven smiled down at him.

"It is I who have misused it, then," he said. "Without mativil my son would have died. He is not just any child on Earth. He is mine, and I am a son of Ormingat."

For some time the machine remained silent, as if its thought banks were constructing some very complex algorithm.

Steven too was thinking of what to say next. He knew what needed to be said, but he was anxious to find the proper words. He laid the baby gently down on a cushion in the corner of the sofa. They were in the half of the ship that was Earth-simulated, a room that could have been in any ordinary English house. There was even a standard lamp behind the sofa, a bookcase full of earthly books, and a small round table where one might sit to eat a meal. On the floor were rugs just like those you have at home.

The other half of the ship was pure laboratory, almost empty, but with the suggestion that necessary things could be made to appear at short notice and occupy the space. The only permanent features were the green cube high up in the dome of the ship, and a great disc that seemed to lie below the level that one's feet might reach. This disc was a clock of stars, a dial with bright points of light over which a wand swung like a single pointer.

The green cube ceased to throb and went totally blank for at least half a minute. Then it glowed clear again.

You have broken rule.

On one level Steven was still puzzling what to say; on a second level his mind came up with: *That's not much of a return on all your thinking, oh voice of Ormingat!* He had enough sense not to say it, of course. Instead, he pulled his own thoughts together and gave them expression.

"What I have done," he said, "I have done for love. And now, because Jacob has come with me into this ship and has diminished just as I have, he must be recognized as Ormingatrig. Otherwise the risk of returning to the outside world would be too great. Entwine him with his name, I beg you."

You have broken rule.

Steven had a sudden, sickening fear that the communicator had somehow crashed under the effort of solving a problem beyond its capability. Was this cube failure? He hoped and prayed that it wasn't. His baby was asleep in the corner of the sofa. His wife was in bed in Whittington Hospital, totally unaware of what was happening. The science of Ormingat must not fail!

So it was with relief that he heard the Cube grate out the words: *What would you?*

"Give my child an Ormingat name. Entwine him with it. He has the right. I have presented him."

Sterekanda, said the communicator, with heavy emphasis upon Steven's Ormingat name in token of the seriousness of this request, *what you ask is a distortion.*

Steven reminded himself that this was a machine after all, however well stocked its data banks. One does not argue with machines; one presses on regardless. Just as they, for their part, obey inner circuits and hear only what has been taught to them.

"My son's Earth name is Jacob," said Steven as coolly as he could. "What will you call him in the Ormingat tongue? With what name will you entwine him?"

Steven picked the child up from the cushion, unwrapped the shawl, and held Jacob up to the Cube as if he were being presented in the temple. The child awoke and his thin, bare arms swayed about above his head, like weeds in water. He did not cry.

From green, the Cube turned to gray and then to yellow. That signaled a great computer dipping back into an even greater system. That was the path of entwining. Steven saw it and knew.

"His Earth name is Jacob," he said with increased confidence. "Tell me his name on Ormingat."

The Cube paused as if undecided, the waves on its surface flattening out into long undulations.

"Give me his name," said Steven steadily, "his Ormingat name."

He is Javayl, throbbed the machine reluctantly, *child of the broken word. He is Javayl, the outsider.*

4

At that moment an orb of silver light surrounded the child and he floated free from his father's arms. Steven knew a moment of terror till the baby was returned to him. He had never witnessed an entwining before, but he knew that this was what he was witnessing now.

In the maternity ward at Whittington Hospital, Lydia slept, knowing nothing of Steven's actions. They had been told, very gently, that their baby was in grave danger of dying. All that could be done would be done, but hopes were not high. Lydia had been allowed to hold the child very briefly in her arms, and the sadness was unbearable. He looked so perfect that it was incredible he should be so ill.

"I'd like to keep him with me," she said. "Just a little longer."

But the masked nurse shook her head and, taking the infant gently back into her gloved hands, she placed him in the tent that was to be his protection for however long he might survive. "That would only put him at greater risk, Mrs. Bradwell," she said sadly. "He must be kept in isolation."

They wheeled Lydia away to her own bed in the ward. She looked back over her shoulder toward the cot and her eyes were blurred with tears.

Two hours later, Steven had gone into the nursery, unobserved, unobservable, and removed his baby from the incubator. He wrapped him in the shawl brought from home for the purpose and simply walked out of the nursery, out of the ward, and into the night. No one stopped him. No one noticed the empty cot. No one would notice it. That was the power of Ormingat, even stronger in Steven than in the other visitors to Earth. Deflection was, after all, an important part of his job.

His return would be just as simple. Then the baby would be seen again, mysteriously fit and well.

*

You are released. Now you must go.

Steven turned to face the center of the rear wall on the Earth side of the ship. This was familiar ground, a situation he had encountered many times over the past three years. A semicircular door opened fanlike, and from the opening the pull, as of a magnet, drew them toward it. Then, with a rush, Steven and the child were sucked out into the night. Up through a layer of soil they went, out into the air of North London, onto the wall of a cemetery. For a few seconds they were no more than tiny dots on the weathered old brick at the base of a rusty railing.

Then the dots flew through the air and increased in size till they became a man holding a baby in his arms. Steven was now standing in Swains Lane, just outside the cemetery. It was nine o'clock on a cool autumn evening. All he had to do now was take the child back to the hospital and return him to his cot as if he had never been away.

CHAPTER 1

Jacob's Birthday

It was Jacob's thirteenth birthday. In many ways it was no different from all his previous birthdays. They didn't hold a disco at the local club and invite dozens of friends from school. Jacob had no friends. He appeared to want no friends. There was his family—his father, his mother, and his two young sisters, Beth and Josie. That was enough.

So the birthday party was just a birthday tea, with a quiet sense of special occasion. There were only two guests from the outside world: Uncle Mark, Lydia's only brother, her elder by some ten years, and his daughter, Molly. They had come, as always, to deliver a card and a present. They needed no invitation and they knew they would find the family at home. Mark's wife stayed away and sent her excuses.

The white cloth with its deep lace edging was brought out especially for party time. Lydia had baked scones and sausage rolls and made mountains of sandwiches. There were cream cakes from the local bakery and an iced birthday cake with thirteen blue candles. The leftovers, no doubt, would fill many baskets!

Greetings had been exchanged and, with the exception of Beth and Josie, everyone was sitting around waiting for the feast to begin.

Uncle Mark smiled across at Jacob. "So now you are a teenager," he said. "We'll have to treat you like a grown-up!"

"What do you treat a grown-up like, Dad?" said Molly, who was only eleven but slick with it. The question was not asked in all innocence. She was already a dab hand at making fun of her father and the silly things he was apt to do and say. "Will Jacob be able to drink wine and stop out late?"

"I don't want to drink wine and stop out late," said Jacob impatiently. "I want to be spoken to as if what I had to say mattered. I want to be accorded . . ."—he blushed—"intellectual equality."

Mark laughed. His laugh was kindly enough, but to Jacob his manner was insulting. In appearance Mark resembled his sister, but he was far more robust and extrovert. His complexion was rosier and his fair hair was inclined to curl.

"They teach you some big words at that school of yours," he said.

"See what I mean?" said Jacob, turning to his father.

Steven smiled at Mark mockingly. They were a complete contrast. Steven's dark hair was brushed straight back from his forehead. His eyes were the deepest brown. But it was not just in coloring that they differed: Steven was much brighter than his brother-in-law, and not always kindly with it!

"I do see what you mean, my son," he said, as if talking only to Jacob, "but maybe Uncle Mark would rather you opted for a place on the junior rugby team. Scrum half, or something like that?"

"Jacob couldn't play rugby," said Molly scornfully before her father could make any retort. "He can't even run as fast as me. And he's useless at catching."

"I don't want to play rugby," said Jacob patiently. "My brains are not in my boots."

"That's soccer," said Mark, trying to turn the conversation into a joke. "In rugby we mostly run with the ball, not kick it!"

It seemed to him that Jacob had the knack of making people feel uncomfortable. He was always such an outsider. Not like his sisters: Beth and Josie were sturdy little Girl Guides, popular with everybody, and full of fun. They were twins, fair like all their mother's family, with light blue eyes and bright, eager smiles. They were eight years old, not particularly clever, but not stupid either.

"Where are the twins?" said Molly.

"At dancing class," said Lydia as she came in from the kitchen carrying yet another tray of food. "They should be back any minute. Kerry from next door takes them."

She set the tray down on the dining table and found spaces for the plates. Then back to the kitchen again for a jug of apple juice and a pot of tea.

"Come on, then," she said. "Let's all have tea."

"What about the twins?" said Molly, giving her aunt an accusing look. "We can't start without them. It wouldn't be fair."

"I think that's them now," said Steven, hurrying to open the door. And sure enough in came the girls, with Kerry from next door right behind them.

"Come and join us," said Lydia to Kerry. "We're having a birthday tea for Jacob. He's thirteen today."

"No, Mrs. Bradwell—no, thank you. I really have to be getting home," said the sixteen-year-old. Then she turned to Jacob and said, "Happy birthday, Jacob."

Without the prompting, she would never have noticed him. She hardly ever did. As for Jacob, he just shrugged his shoulders and made no reply.

So it was just the family who sat down to tea.

"Aunt Jane will be sorry she's missed this," said Mark, observing how well they all looked as a family, "but you know how things are."

"She's got another headache," said Molly. "My mother is always getting headaches."

"Have a sausage roll," said Lydia hastily. Molly was a precocious child with little sense of loyalty.

Steven, Lydia, and Jacob had little to say as they sat at the table. Lydia and her son were never talkative. Steven, as usual, had little patience with Mark. So silence was best. Beth and Josie more than made up for the rest of the Bradwells. They ate a lot, talked a lot, and then took Molly to their room to see an array of Barbie dolls dressed in every style you could think of.

Jacob was about to make his getaway when Uncle Mark cried, "Hey, not so fast! You haven't opened your present yet."

Jacob smiled weakly and turned to the box that was lying on the floor. Opening presents was always a worry. What if he didn't like what was inside? Last year it had been a football strip two sizes too large. This year it looked as if it might be a football. But, credit where credit is due, when Jacob removed the wrapping and opened the box, what he took out was at least original, though not exactly welcome.

"Well?" said his uncle, smiling expectantly. "It's a genuine model spaceship. You can open it up and see the whole works in-side. There's even a battery to produce flashing lights."

Lydia gave her son a warning glance. Steven put one hand quite heavily on Jacob's shoulder. "Maybe you'd like to take it to your room," he said. "I know I always like to examine stuff like that on my own, gives you more chance to get to know it."

"Yes, I will," said Jacob. "Thanks, Uncle Mark. See you later."

"No, no," said Mark. "We'll have to be going shortly. Don't want to miss the train. You go off and enjoy yourself. Don't worry about using up the batteries—I've put a spare pack in to keep you going."

When Steven and Lydia were alone again, Steven said, "How does he do it? I mean, he's got Molly—and Michael's seventeen now. How does he not realize that a thirteen-year-old doesn't play with toys like that?"

"Some do," said Lydia, trying to be fair. "Jacob's always been old for his age. And it must have been quite expensive."

The present also made Steven feel uncomfortable in quite a different way. It reminded him that there were things he should discuss with Jacob—things about a real spaceship resting in the soil in Highgate Cemetery. It was smaller than the toy Jacob had carried to his room, but much more functional. Four years from now, it would complete its mission and shoot off into outer space.

"I think I'll see if Jacob would like to go for a walk," said Steven.

"At this time?" said Lydia. "It's nearly dark and turning chilly."

"We can wrap up well," said Steven. "I need a walk and I think he does too."

Lydia was quite used to Steven and his evening rambles. On the whole, she approved of them. It did him good to get away from the computer desk. But to take Jacob with him was something new. New, and pleasing.

"Don't expect too much intellectual equality," she said with a smile. "He knows the words, but I don't know if he quite appreciates what they mean."

Steven was momentarily startled. It was as if Lydia had read his mind. She couldn't, of course. After all these years, she still knew nothing.

CHAPTER 2

Into the Night

They walked quickly, in step, out of their own little street, then down Chester Road and up nearly to the top of Swains Lane. There was no one about this chilly evening. This was not part of the city that never sleeps. The school and the library were in darkness. The gate of the cemetery was shut; lamplight lit up the ivy growing about its walls.

By the time Steven and Jacob reached their destination, it was already dark. They talked from time to time, but Steven did not mention the spaceship. He concentrated upon other things.

"Are you happy, Jacob?" was one question.

"Why do you ask?" said Jacob, almost aggressively.

"It's not a question I have ever asked you before," said his father. "I always think it's a pointless question to put to a child. But if we are to be equals, I feel I can ask it now."

"And I can wonder why you think I'm not," said Jacob, prepared now at least to talk round the question. "You must think that I am somehow short on happiness, or you wouldn't bother to ask."

"True," said his father. "I am asking because you have always seemed to me to be too isolated, and I blame myself."

"I don't see how you can do that," said Jacob. "I am a bit of an outsider, but I've figured out that must be part of my makeup.

Everybody's different. It's not your fault. And I can't say it makes me desperately unhappy. It's just one of those things."

Jacob felt uncomfortable with this conversation. Loneliness did trouble him, but he would never tell anyone, not even his father. He knew, only too well he knew, what it was to go unnoticed, to be forgotten, to seem totally invisible. And it hurt.

What hurt most was the strangeness of not being like other people, when there was nothing he could pinpoint that made him different. He was of average height and build, his coloring attractive rather than otherwise—a sallow complexion, perhaps, but he had fine, dark eyes and good, even features. In fact, he strongly resembled his father. Nothing in his appearance could account for the way in which everyone he met simply ignored him.

"It might be my fault," said Steven cautiously, not looking directly at the boy but directing his glance through the railing at an obelisk, beneath which was buried not only a famous man but also, at a lesser depth and at its outer rim, a spaceship from the planet Ormingat.

Jacob glanced sideways at his father. "Genes?" he said. "Heredity?"

"Not as easy as that," said his father. "You are different because you are my son."

"Beth and Josie are your daughters," said Jacob with a smile as he thought of his noisy, bubbly sisters. "No one could ever say that they were in any way isolated."

"They were not presented," said his father. "You were."

"Presented?"

"If I had not presented you, Javayl ban," said Steven anxiously, "you would have died. I had no choice."

The pronouncement of the Ormingat name, in vibrating Ormingat tones, made Jacob shiver; his arms prickled and the hairs grew stiff on the back of his neck. He had known the story of his infancy: the recovery that no one could explain. Till now he had accepted it as a gift from God. That anyone on Earth had played an active part in this miracle was beyond imagination. Yet now, as he heard his Ormingat name for the very first time, he experienced some sort of recognition.

"Explain," he said tersely.

"Not here," said Steven. "Out here in the open air of a London street, with evidence of humanity, living and dead, on every side, I would not know how to tell it, and you would find it impossible to believe."

"Where, then?"

Steven took from his coat pocket an old steel ruler, which he unfolded to its full length. He grinned at Jacob, saying, "Not the latest technology—but effective improvisation."

Jacob stared at him, uncomprehending. There they were, standing nearly at the top of Swains Lane, outside the rusty railings of the cemetery, and his father's words about technology were too cryptic to mean anything at all. What in the world was he talking about? Why in the world were they here?

Steven put the ruler through the railings. Then he bent it at its topmost joint so that the first segment straddled the crumbling brick wall and the rest of the ruler went diagonally down into the cemetery. "Now you must hold my hand," said Steven. He stretched one hand out behind him for his son to clutch.

"One question," said Jacob, refusing to be fazed by all this strangeness. "What is your name? If I am Javaylban, who then are you?"

Steven turned from the wall, the ruler still in his hand. It was an Ormingat question. An Earth child would have been asking other questions at this point.

"You are Javayl. I suppose ban is a term of endearment—love of a parent for a child. I am Sterekanda. Now, quickly, take my hand and let's waste no more time. Just trust me."

Jacob looked at his father's face, so like his own, high-cheekboned, fine-featured, with eyes thick-lashed and dark. "I do trust you, Dad, though what you are planning to do with an old steel ruler is a mystery to me. Is it some sort of joke?"

"Trust me, *Javayl ban*," said Steven urgently. "Take hold of my hand and trust me."

"I trust you, *Sterekanda ban*," said Jacob, trying hard to be trustful but feeling mainly doubt. He held out his right hand toward his father's left.

The words were not quite right, but the accent and intonation were perfect—even the voice had an unearthly sound. Jacob had a rare talent for listening and imitating.

"*Sterekanda mesht*," said Steven softly. "That is what the child says to the parent. Now, come."

Javayl grasped his father's hand, not knowing what would happen next, but convinced that something would.

From her turret window in the mansion block above Swains Lane, a very old lady looked out into the dusk. One heavily ringed hand, wrinkled and clawlike, held back a long velvet curtain. Lady Maudleigh was caught in a frozen moment. She had paused there much earlier to watch for the Friese-Greene fox, as she liked to call it. If she was lucky, just at sunset, she would catch a glimpse of the little animal doing a sharp leap in front of the obelisk, his bright eyes occasionally catching the light from the streetlamp. It was an exciting thing to see in the city of the dead. The clustered graves, mainly hidden by trees and undergrowth, held for her neither fear nor misery. She had known them too long, and loved them too well. They were at peace.

But tonight, before she came out of her reverie to close the curtains, a man and a boy came and stood close by the cemetery railings, just in front of the obelisk. They had their backs to her, as if peering in at the graves. Her ladyship's nose pressed childishly against the windowpane. What were those two doing there? They must be up to something. She hoped they would not harm or frighten the fox. She watched them anxiously.

Then, as if by magic, the strangers disappeared. One second they were there; the next they were gone!

Lady Maudleigh shook her head vigorously. "You imagined that, Theresa!" she said to herself. "You can't possibly have seen what you thought you saw!"

She shivered nevertheless. Then she pulled the cord that drew the curtains and very firmly shut out the night.

CHAPTER 3

Revelations

The tip of the ruler barely touched the soil. That was enough. The ship's sensors detected it and knew who was holding it. With the speed of lightning, the man and the boy rapidly diminished until they were invisible to the human eye.

Jacob felt the weird sensation of somehow being pulled from without and from within. A great dizziness overcame him and he closed his eyes. When next he opened them, he was seated on a sofa in a very strange room.

"We've arrived, *Javayl ban*," said his father, taking the boy by both hands now and trying to project reassurance. "Now is the time for me to explain."

Jacob looked around the room. Half of it was an ordinary living room, comfortable and neat, but with books scattered here and there, and a lived-in look about it. The other half was impossible to understand; its proportions were all wrong, as if its "half" were somehow infinitely bigger.

"That is what I call the laboratory," said Steven, nodding toward it.

High up on one side of this space, under the slope of the dome, was a green, opalescent cube. On the floor of the "laboratory," deep down, ticking softly with the rhythm of a clock, was a huge disc covered in stars. Its face was dark blue velvet.

Points of jewel-like light spun across it. A wand three-quarters full of gleaming lights turned as on a pivot round the disc's equator. It was the most wonderful, mystical thing that Jacob had ever seen.

"Where are we?" he said, turning to his father. "Where are we, and how did we get here?"

"See my hands?" said Steven, cupping his hands together as if holding a ball.

"Yes," said Jacob doubtfully.

"We are inside a ball that in the outside world I could hold like this in the palms of my hands. That ball is the spaceship that brought me here."

Jacob gave him a look of disbelief.

"Outside view! Action replay!" snapped Steven, flicking his fingers at the Cube. It turned from green to silver and then gave a complete rerun of what had happened just seconds before. The man held the steel rule; the boy held the man's hand. Then man and boy and rule seemed to dissolve into nothingness.

"We disappeared?" said Jacob, recognizing himself and his father and the very street where they had stood.

"No," said Steven. "We simply diminished and became the size required for these surroundings. And, before you ask, no, I am not a magician. This is pure science—Ormingat science, *Javayl ban.*"

The Cube, which had turned to green again, selected this moment to speak.

It was time to bring the boy. How much has he been told?

The voice spoke in English, but its tone and accent were not of this world.

Jacob felt a shiver run down his spine at the sudden sound of this robotic voice. He stared first at the Cube and then at his father. What was coming next? What *could* come next?

"Till this evening," said Steven to the Cube, "he knew nothing, except perhaps in his deepest soul. Today is my son's thirteenth birthday, by Earth reckoning. It was time to make him acquainted with his origins."

How much has he been told?

"He knows he is Javayl and that he is very special."

Take time. Tell him more. Tell him all he needs to know.

The Cube then went totally blank, its surfaces an oily, phlegmish gray.

Steven knew what that meant: he was to be left alone with his explanations. So, in as few words as possible, he told Jacob of his own journey from Ormingat, a faraway planet in a different solar system.

". . . And I landed in Highgate Cemetery, just inside the wall. It was not exactly where I was meant to land, but near enough for me to find my way. My preparation was superb. I had the speech of this land and the map of this location firmly in my brain. I was Steven Bradwell, a young man with a whole Earth background etched in around him. But the true me is Sterekanda, and I remain an alien on this planet."

"And I am half alien?" said Jacob, ever quick in his deductions.

"No," said his father. "You remain your mother's son, of course, but you are totally alien: that is what happened when you were entwined with your name."

"So that is why I have always felt so set apart?"

The Cube glowed green again. It had detected a truth about the boy. Javayl appeared to be standing in the faintest of shadows.

Not so. Ormingatrig are not necessarily isolated. You were overprotected. Mistakes can be made. Sterekanda made one in ordering your life so.

Steven looked puzzled and then annoyed.

"I had to protect him," he protested. "No one must ever hurt him."

It is you who have hurt him. You put such a cloak of protection between him and the world that he escaped not just harm but all possibility of happiness.

Jacob turned on his father and his look demanded an explanation before he could even put a question into words.

"What was the cloak of protection? What did you do to me?"

"I surrounded you with love," said his father helplessly. "We were so near to losing you."

Tell him the truth.

"That is the truth," said Steven. "I never lie."

It is not whole truth.

"So what is the whole truth, Dad? What are you keeping back from me?"

He surrounded you with science.

That didn't make sense either. Steven's office at the top of the house was full of computer equipment, not to be touched by the family. That was the nearest they came to anything that could be called science.

"Well?" said Jacob, giving his father a harsh look.

"At home," said Steven, "among my earthly computer stuff, there is the item we always call the Brick. Remember?"

"Yes," said Jacob. "It is orange and shiny and has buttons set in its faces, but it does look a bit like a builder's brick. That's why we gave it the name."

"It is not Earth equipment. It came with me from the Faraway Planet. It is my responsibility and the source of my power."

"Power to do what?" said Jacob suspiciously.

"Power to direct attention away from anyone or anything that needs such protection. It is highly specialized and very sophisticated. That, I suppose, is why it was such fun to call it a brick!"

Steven smiled, but Jacob was not smiling.

"You directed attention away from me!" he said, outraged. "You made sure that I would never be noticed."

"No one ever hurt you," said Steven defensively. "No one ever teased or bullied you."

"No one ever *knew* me," said his son, and for the first time since

20

infancy he began to cry, letting out tears that had been held back for years.

You have much to make up, Sterekanda.

"I will," said Steven, grasping the boy's hands in his. "I truly will."

To withdraw the shield will not do. You have left it too late for that.

Steven shivered. "What can I do, then?" he asked, with unusual humility.

Give him a full part to play in your life. Let him share in the work of Ormingat. Whenever you come to the ship, make sure that he comes too.

"I will," said Steven. Then he said, in self-defense, "His sisters know him and love him. His mother dotes on him. There has been no shield within the family home."

There could not have been, even had you so desired.

As they walked home, Jacob was lost in bewildered thought. It was all so impossible. What had just happened to his own body filled him with a sense of unreality. Because, throughout his short life, he had been so little recognized or accepted by the outside world, his home and his family were all and everything to him. Now that safe little boat had been well and truly rocked.

"What about Mum?" he asked. "How much does she know?"

They were at the corner of Chester Road, making ready to cross. A cyclist came out of Holly Village just as Jacob spoke. Steven gripped his son's arm and they both stood back. He did not speak until the rider was well past. That gave him time to consider what to say.

"Your mother is so important a part of my life," he said eventually, "that sometimes I think she must really know everything."

"What have you told her?" said Jacob, knowing that he could not take these words at face value.

"Nothing," said Steven.

"Then she knows nothing," said Jacob sternly.

Steven smiled wanly. In all the years of his married life he had never been tempted to tell Lydia anything about his other self. The rules of Ormingat would have forbidden it, naturally, but Steven had little respect for the rules. He had great love for Lydia and a fear of saying or doing anything that might destroy her fragile happiness.

"There are levels of knowledge," he said to Jacob, avoiding a straightforward discussion. "Words are not everything. Your mother knows me as I am. She is a very special person."

No one will ever know me, thought Jacob bitterly. *That is something you have made sure of.* He clenched his fists and his eyes stung with tears.

Steven put an arm around his shoulders, uncertain how to comfort him.

"You'll be my helper now," he said. "This has brought you closer to me. There is a lot to learn and I want to teach you. Take it all slowly. It will come right, *Javayl ban.*"

"Will it? Will it, *Sterekanda?*"

He could have said *Sterekanda mesht,* but preferred to leave off the endearment. The omission was not lost on his father.

CHAPTER 4

Saturday Morning

Lydia was mixing a cake. She mixed at a leisurely pace as if tomorrow would do, which it would. The mother of the Bradwell family was not a methodical housewife. If she took it in mind to bake a cake, that is what she would do. Yesterday's feast had not included a homemade cake. But today the bowl on the shelf had managed to catch her attention, and there were still eggs left in the fridge.

Her long, fair hair was pulled back severely to protect the cooking from unwanted strands. The slim hand that held the wooden spoon moved to the rhythm of the tune she was humming under her breath. The face inside her soul was very delicate and beautiful. The face she showed the world was heavy-jawed and quite plain, made plainer by the drawn-back hair and the lips that were closely sealed in tuneful thought.

Jacob looked at his mother, seeing only the face of her soul. Young as he was, he knew she was vulnerable and felt that somehow she needed protection.

How did you come to marry my father?

This was the question he wanted to ask, but couldn't. There was always a reticence, a fear of saying something that would hurt too much.

Lydia looked across at him. He was sitting on a high stool beside the breakfast bar. She was standing by the table that was the

23

pride of her kitchen, a scrubbable table with a top made of planks of plain, white wood. She smiled.

Beneath the smile there was the expectation that her son would have something to say. He had seemed even more withdrawn than usual when he and his father returned from their walk the night before. But, being Lydia, she would not press for any confidence. Reticence was part of her code and deeply rooted in her character.

"I make wonderful cakes," she said quite simply. "This one will be really special."

Jacob returned the smile with a grin that hid what he was feeling.

"We fed well yesterday," he said. "Is this getting to be a habit?"

"Cheeky!" said Lydia. "If you're not careful, I won't let you scrape the bowl!"

Was now the moment to ask the question?

How did you come to marry my father?

No, thought Jacob, now was definitely not the time. There never would be a time when the question could be asked. The mystery of how this shy, retiring Earthling, comfortable only within the confines of her own home, came to be the wife of an alien would never be resolved.

Jacob watched her in silence as she carefully turned the cake mixture into the greased tin.

"Do you never think of doing other things, of being different?" he asked. This was as near as he could come to approaching the subject nearest to his heart at that moment.

"I am happy as I am," said Lydia. "This is the life of my choosing. I was lucky to be given the choice."

She turned to open the oven door and over her shoulder she added, "And the main ingredient in this cake is love. That's what makes it taste so good."

There was nothing more to be said. How much did she know?

How much had she guessed? How much was just buried deep in her heart? Jacob longed to know, but asking was impossible.

Beth and Josie came into the kitchen together, bouncing noisily through a door more suited to one than to two.

"Can we help Kerry this morning?"

"Can we go with her to walk the dog?"

"She's got another dog. It's called Mitsubishi."

"I don't know how Mrs. McKinley manages with all those animals!" said Lydia. Their neighbors had two or maybe three cats, a parrot, and two brown rabbits. Their old dog, Leonora, had recently died. The twins were clearly excited about the new one.

"Mitsubishi wants us to go. He's real fun and sometimes he gets away on the heath and Kerry has to catch him. And we can help. He's just a puppy."

"When he grows up, he might be a giraffe."

"Ye-es?" said their mother, pausing in the act of cleaning the wooden spoon.

"Well, that's what Kerry says!"

"And is there nothing else you should be doing?" said Lydia. "You don't want to leave all your homework till the last minute."

"I finished all of mine in bed, Mum. I have no more left to do."

"You didn't," said her twin. "I finished it—you just copied what I wrote."

"I understood it, anyway," said the other. "That's the main thing. If Mrs. Potts wants to know about—"

"Hush!" said their mother, her hands conducting their sound into silence. "You'll spoil my cake. It is there in the oven trying hard to be beautiful. If it hears you two, it will probably collapse in the middle!"

The twins gave each other a look. No one they knew talked quite like their mother. And often it didn't make sense.

Jacob had been sitting quietly, scraping the mixture from the bowl. Now he spoke. "Mitsubishi's a daft name for a dog," he said.

"No, it's not," said his sisters delightedly. "Do you want to know why he's called Mitsubishi?"

"All right," said Jacob, aware that a weak joke must be coming. "Let's have a groan. Why is the dog called Mitsubishi?"

"Because," said the girls in unison, "there are already too many dogs called Rover."

"My poor cake," said Lydia in mock despair. "What is it going to make of all this?"

"So we can go now?"

"Yes, you can go. Be back by half twelve. And put on your boots—the grass is sure to be wet."

After they'd gone, Lydia got out the ironing board.

"I think I'll iron some shirts," she said, pulling out the blue basket from under the table. "That way I'll be on hand and won't forget there's a cake in the oven. It would be sad if I spoilt it after putting so much effort in!"

Without being asked, Jacob got up and fixed the clotheshorse ready to receive the ironed washing.

"Thanks," said Lydia. "Now I can have a nice warm morning in my nice warm kitchen listening to the radio."

"And I think I'll go and see what Dad's doing. I heard him go up to the computer room," said Jacob.

So he left without making a single reference to aliens, without finding out any more than he already knew.

Lydia plugged in the iron and stood it on its heel while she arranged a shirt on the ironing board. She switched on the radio, which had its usual Saturday mix of familiar music. This was the heart of the home. Stories took over her mind; memories drifted in and out.

CHAPTER 5

Saturday Afternoon

When Jacob entered the computer room, he felt strangely shy. It was a room he had visited many times before. He had even been shown how to use the computer—the "Earth" computer. But today the place had lost all its old familiarity. He felt as if he had never been there before.

Yesterday had been the most fantastic day of Jacob's life. He had become part of something that all his earthly knowledge would have rejected as totally impossible. It wasn't a dream—he knew that for certain—but it felt dreamlike.

Steven was working on his ordinary, Earth computer, creating a program for a purely human client, when Jacob came in. He half turned, absently gestured to the camp stool beside the desk where the Brick was lodged, and motioned to his son to sit down.

It was a large room with a long window under the eaves of the house. The ceiling sloped steeply. The floor of polished wood was partly covered with two large rugs. On the wall to the right of the door was a little, old iron fireplace that housed a two-bar electric fire. The desk that held the Brick was against the wall to the left of the door. The Earth computer stood on a long, cluttered table beneath the window. And, in between, the remaining wall space was filled with shelves from floor to ceiling.

"I won't be a minute," said Steven. "Just let me finish this bit.

I know we have things to talk about. Let's take our time and talk."

Jacob sat in uncomfortable silence for a while. He looked at the Brick from time to time, seeing it with different eyes now that he knew more of its history. It did not look like any other computer he had ever seen. The brick shape gave it a heavy appearance, as if it were made of real brick, and certainly not of any sort of plastic. Its buttons were colorful and looked stuck on rather than embedded. Its screen, which he had seen before, was furled up out of sight. It had no recognizable monitor. Jacob had never been allowed to touch this instrument. For a second or two he felt tempted to let his fingers slide a little lever at the base of it, or maybe just gently push the scarlet button.

"No!" said his father without even turning his head. "That could be dangerous!"

Jacob blushed and drew back. Steven remained hunched over and busy for a few more minutes. The window had no curtains. The sun was slanting in on him.

Jacob saw him ease back on his chair and stretch out his arms. It was only then that he ventured to speak.

"I tried to talk to Mum today," he said in a very strained voice, glad somehow that he was saying this to the back of his father's head.

"I imagine you talk to your mother most days," said Steven, tightening up, ready for what might follow. He swiveled round in his chair to face his son.

"I wanted to ask her how much she knew," said Jacob. It was not necessary to be more specific. Each knew what the other meant.

"And?" said his father.

"I couldn't," said Jacob. "Whenever I was on the brink of saying something, I was held back."

Steven let out a sigh. "Good," he said. "That has to do with the fencing."

Jacob waited to hear what his father would say next. He refused to be led on to asking any more questions. He still resented the thirteen years of silence. For thirteen years one of the most important facts of his life had been withheld from him. *So, he thought sullenly, tell me, or don't tell me. It's up to you.*

"You see," his father continued, after an almost painful pause, "there are certain subjects that are fenced about. Neither you nor anybody on Earth is permitted to probe into them too far."

Jacob thought fast. Before his father could construct any more "fences," he blurted out the words, "Why did you marry my mother? How did you meet her?"

Steven was startled by the questions, but he managed a smile, a mischievous smile. "I found her standing barefoot outside in the snow," he said. "She was striking matches in an effort to keep herself warm."

Jacob looked angry. "Why talk such rubbish?" he snapped. "I ask you a sensible question and you try to make out she's the Little Matchgirl. Uncle Mark is her brother. My grandmother was still alive when I was born. Mum was never alone or neglected."

"She was not neglected," said Steven, "but she was often alone. She was alone at the concert hall where I first met her. She looked lost. She told me later that she had been trying to be like everybody else but couldn't quite manage it!"

He put one hand on his son's shoulder and gave him a look that was serious and penetrating.

"I was speaking in metaphor, Javayl," he said. "There are waif-souls in this universe. Your mother is one such. And I—I have great love for the waif-soul. Do you understand?"

"And is my soul a waif?" said Jacob, knowing only too well what loneliness was.

"Who knows?" said his father, unwilling to discuss it further. "Who really knows anything?"

He turned abruptly to the computer and typed in a few more

lines before turning to face his son again. He had decided to tell Jacob another story, a true one.

"The tale I told you has a basis in reality. Your mother did once stand outside the window one snowy January afternoon when dark had just fallen and the house was lit up but the curtains were open. She had taken off her shoes and was standing out there in just a party dress. She was eight years old at the time. She wanted to see what it felt like to be the Little Matchgirl. So she stood there, striking matches till she was caught."

"How do you know that?" asked Jacob.

"She told me, or at least I think she told me."

"Didn't she catch pneumonia?"

"No," said Steven with a smile. "I think she caught a spanking and was sent to bed!"

Jacob decided that there was no point in pursuing the question any further, but he did say resentfully, "You are wrong about the so-called fencing."

"What do you mean by 'wrong'?" said Steven haughtily. "You know nothing about it."

Jacob stood up to leave.

"I failed to question my mother," he said, "because I couldn't bear to hurt her. That failure had nothing at all to do with you or any power of Ormingat."

CHAPTER 6

Working with Dad

Steven was determined to make things right with his son. To Lydia's surprise, he spent more and more time talking to him, explaining about computers, even playing family games he had formerly disdained—"old-fashioned" games like Scrabble and Monopoly. The girls joined in, of course, and found it fun.

But when Steven took Jacob to work in the computer room, the others were not invited. That was accepted by everyone. It was as if Jacob had started on an apprenticeship, ready to take over the family business.

The early days were the best. Everything was so amazing. Jacob watched with wonder as his father set the Brick to work. Steven always worked from instructions, like a job sheet. He used his special skills to do what others told him needed to be done. If some operative from Ormingat required special protection of the type the Brick could provide, Steven would find him or her on the map, would study the circumstances, and then would do what was required. The Brick was able to search, to find, and then, on Steven's considered decision, to protect from notice.

At the touch of a button, a screen would roll upward on a frame to a vertical position above the Brick. It was the size of a sheet of A4 paper, laid horizontally. Steven could produce on the screen the map of any area in Europe. He could home in on a single house in a single street. Then the Brick's viewer could enter the house and focus on any object in any room. The Ormingatrig observers were here on Earth in a variety of places with a variety of personas. Some had an easy time of it; others found themselves in situations where the power of the Brick was often a dire necessity.

"Harsheelin needs our assistance," said Steven as he focused on a little shop in Amsterdam where something decidedly strange was made to happen to an exceptionally fine diamond. It was in its velvet tray on a glass counter. Two thieves entered the shop as Harsheelin stood by, helpless. In his Earth persona, Harsheelin was a diamond merchant dealing in fine stones. It was his mission to learn about and report upon what this world most valued.

In came the thieves, both masked and armed. Harsheelin froze. The two men looked round vaguely, and then walked out again without seeing either the man or the stone.

Jacob watched them wandering in and then out of the shop like drunken sailors, and gave a laugh.

"There now," said Steven. "Our man is well protected. Those two will be well and truly bewildered when they make their get-away!"

"You did that?" said Jacob. "That was sensational!"

"That was easy," said Steven. "It isn't always as easy as that. We have to be put on the right track. Other Ormingatrig have to supply the information, which is relayed to me. I never meet them or talk to them. That's the rule. I have not yet found it necessary to break it!"

Jacob's cleverness stopped short of understanding his father's humor. When Steven's lips curled in a smile and his eyes twinkled, it was a mixture of self-mockery and impudence. His name, after all, was Sterekanda, which in his own tongue meant "rule breaker," the name playfully but prophetically given to him by his parents in his infancy.

"It is the Brick that protects me, isn't it?" said Jacob one day, when he had had time to assimilate all that was happening.

Steven nodded.

"Withdraw the protection," said Jacob. "I don't need it anymore."

Steven had just enough sensitivity to look regretful.

"It's too late. You have been surrounded by the shield for so long that I don't know what would happen if I attempted to withdraw it."

Jacob clenched his fists, but said no more. His own self-knowledge made him accept that what his father said was true, however much he might hate it.

Steven still kept secrets from his son. At no time did Jacob ask about his father's return to Ormingat. At no time did he ever ask anything about the great disc that ticked like a clock on the spaceship's floor. The questions were fenced off from him. He was never permitted to wonder about them. That was part of his father's power: the ability to deflect attention. The Brick provided total cover from a distance, in limited situations. Steven's own mesmeric capability was more intimate, depending upon close contact, but every bit as powerful.

By the time Jacob reached his fourteenth birthday, at the end of the following October, visits to the computer room had become routine. There had been fewer visits to the spaceship—fewer were called for—but Jacob was by now less in awe of it. The isolation that continued to surround him in the outside world now became a positive asset. There was no friend with whom he would be tempted to share his great secret, or even regret being unable to share. No one knew what he did, and no one cared.

Then, shortly before Christmas, things began to happen that were more than usually interesting.

They first heard the news of it not through the usual channel, a small purple button flashing swiftly in the lower right-hand corner of the Brick, but on terrestrial television. An item at the end of the news told briefly of a strange accident that had happened earlier that day, somewhere in the North of England, leaving a mysterious aftermath. At first, the family were so little interested in it that not even the exact location registered. Casselton—wasn't that someplace in Scotland?

If they had listened properly, they would have known that it was a town in the North of England, where a beer tanker had crashed into a post office van. The two men in the tanker sustained injuries that needed hospital treatment but were not life threatening. The driver of the post office van was badly injured and in the same hospital. A fourth casualty was a boy who was suffering from shock and could not be persuaded to talk.

What drew Steven's attention was the mystery of the disappearing victim. Apparently both men in the tanker were convinced that a pedestrian had been crushed between the tanker and the van. But there was no trace of any body, not even the fragment of a corpse. And the shocked boy's father was, for the moment at least, a missing piece in this odd jigsaw.

Steven felt a shiver run through him. He could not have defined exactly why, but somehow he felt connected to this accident. He came from a world where illusion was part of the system. The apparent disappearance of an accident victim was, for him, within the realm of possibility.

He stretched his arms, stood up, and said casually, "Work to do. Care to join me, Jacob?"

Lydia gave him a curious look.

"I thought you were finished for the day," she said.

"Something I just thought of," said Steven. "Jacob might be interested."

Jacob got up from his armchair, smiled at his mother, and shrugged his shoulders, much as to say, You know what he's like, Mum!

Lydia said nothing more.

Beth and Josie were sitting at the dining table, looking at catalogs of Christmas gifts, wondering what the big day would bring for them. There was just a week to go till Christmas. They were taking no notice of the television and were so used to Jacob and his father working together that their exit did not even break their concentration.

Jacob followed his father up to the computer room. "What is it?" he said as his father opened the door with his key: this room had to be kept locked at all times.

"Something, maybe," said Steven. "Maybe nothing."

But when they went into the darkened room, the purple button on the Brick was flashing furiously.

Steven pressed the button anxiously and pulled the switch that made the screen unfold. On it were just three words:

GO TO SPACESHIP.

No more were needed. Clearly the communicator wanted to convey something that would require more discussion or more information than was usually displayed on the screen.

Jacob looked eagerly at his father. "Do we go now?" he said.

"Oh, yes," said Steven. "When our little friend there says that we must go to see our big friend, he means now, this minute! Get your coat."

"It's awful weather," said Jacob. "Mum won't like us going out in it, just for a walk like that. I mean, we can't tell her anything, can we?"

Steven smiled. "Sometimes I think your mother knows more than any of us and just keeps quiet!"

"It's not very nice out there," said Lydia when they looked into the living room all ready to go.

"We won't be long," said Steven, pulling on his gloves, "and we're well wrapped up."

"But where are you going?" said Lydia.

"No further than the top of the hill," said Steven. "It's just a simple experiment."

"That I wouldn't understand?" said Lydia.

"I wouldn't say that," said Steven quickly. "If you were interested, I am sure you would understand, but communications and such are not really your thing, are they?"

"I suppose not," said Lydia, clearly deciding to make no further attempt to communicate.

"There," said Steven as they closed the door behind them, "not so bad, was it? Your mother has tact beyond average!"

"She might worry," said Jacob, still uncertain. He was still close enough to childhood to know how much trouble Lydia took to ensure that her children were always safe and clean and fed.

"She won't," said Steven, believing what he wanted to believe. "Your mother knows me better than to worry."

CHAPTER 7

I've Never Heard of Him

Despite the weather, and the sense of urgency, they walked up to the cemetery. Their own car would have been an encumbrance, a taxi an embarrassment. They walked quickly and by the time they got there, both were slightly out of breath, and very uncomfortable.

The wind had blown a thin drizzle in their faces all the way up the hill. The night was dark and trees in the cemetery wept needlessly over silent graves. No ghost would come haunting. No one was even watching from a window. Lady Maudleigh had already closed her curtains. As for the fox, he was curled up beneath a shrub, licking a small wound he had collected earlier in the day, and feeling bedraggled and forlorn.

Two living beings had the whole of Swains Lane entirely to themselves.

Steven shivered as he took out the ruler and unfolded it with gloved fingers. To get into the ship, out of the rain's and the wind's way, would be a welcome transition.

Entry was as smooth as usual.

Steven directed Jacob to the sofa and told him to sit quietly and just observe. "This is going to be tricky," he said grimly. "There are too many things I don't know, and I am determined to be told."

Then he moved toward the green Cube. On the panel beneath

it there was one simple lever. He pulled it sharply to the right, into its loop. Before contact was made, Steven knew that this emergency must be connected with the missing accident victim. What puzzled him was that at no time had he been asked to provide help or protection for anyone in the North of England.

Who was located there?

What was this all about?

Agents never met, of course, but it was part of Steven's job to know who they were and to be ready to provide remote assistance. He had never heard of any agent living or working in Casselton.

The green Cube glowed and swiveled on its axis. *Trouble. Great trouble.*

"Yes," said Steven tersely. He sat smoldering, waiting for what was coming next.

One of our observers has diminished.

"We all diminish to enter our spaceships," said Steven icily. "Diminution is part of our system."

One of our observers has diminished.

"Which observer, and where?" said Steven, thinking that this question might work, might spur the sluggish equipment to get on with it.

In Casselton. Vateelin is out of context.

"I have never heard of an agent called Vateelin," said Steven in a voice that threatened subservience. "No warning has been given to me of his arrival. I have made no preparations."

The communicator did not reply. It simply repeated itself. *In Casselton. Vateelin is out of context.*

Steven gave the communicator a baleful look. It was clearly necessary to try another tack. Query *context*? That might work. The communicator generated English that was near perfect. But, unlike the Ormingat agents, it remained a translator and sometimes its translations were less than clear.

Out of context, thought Steven. Yes. This agent must have diminished at the wrong time, in the wrong place. And the wrong place would have to be outside the ship. Outside the ship!

"How is this agent out of context?" said Steven, not really expecting a coherent reply. Talking to the communicator could be a very uphill battle.

But he got one.

Vateelin's Earth body was about to be crushed between two vehicles. We have not encountered this before. It is assumed that when the space between the two vehicles became too small for a human context, his body was informed to diminish.

"But what was he doing there in the first place?" said Steven. "Where should he have been?"

Vateelin was thrown into the air and landed on the windscreen of a car traveling on the opposite side of the road. We must track him, find him, and protect him until the current irregularity can be corrected. That is for you to do.

"I haven't a clue whom you're talking about," said Steven. "You expect me to go and find someone I don't know, in a location that is unspecified, and then do a job that I have never been called upon to do before. No, no, no!"

Yes.

Steven did not speak.

Jacob was on the edge of his seat, waiting for his father to answer. This situation was fantastic, marvelous even. He wanted to know where it would lead. This surely was a very special mission. Yet there was his father, glaring at the Cube and not giving an inch. Jacob had to bite his tongue to hold back his own questions.

First to break the silence was the Cube. It sounded almost conciliatory. *You will be given directions.*

"Directions!" stormed Steven. "I'll need more than directions. I want to know who this character is and why he is here on my patch without my knowledge. Every agent in Western Europe should be known to me. Intelligence does not operate in a vacuum."

The Cube ignored this outburst completely.

The car is a blue Mercedes. It is now at rest in a town called Morpeth. Full details of its identification, exact location, and plate numbers will appear on the screen of the protection module.

Jacob looked at his father doubtfully. The Cube was clearly directing their attention to this car, where presumably the hapless victim of the accident was still lodged. To go on saying no was impossible. The Brick was the protection module—he knew that. So they must return to the Brick.

Steven was still enraged, but rapidly coming to the same conclusion. "Locating the car does not mean that I can locate the man," he said sulkily. "I have never had to find a diminished one on this Earth. It might be impossible."

The communicator ignored this.

Go now.

"I have the right to know more about Vateelin," said Steven in protest. "Who is he? What is he doing here?"

Consult archives.

"Archives?" said Steven. "What is he doing in the archives? How long has this fellow been in my area, for goodness' sake? Why do I know nothing about him? What sort of skulduggery is this?"

Go now. Time is short.

And so, thought Steven, *is your information. And so,* he added to himself irreverently, *is this fellow Vateelin. Why did he have to go and get himself in such a mess? Could he not have watched where he was going?*

Jacob got up and clutched his father's hand. If time was short, the spaceship would be swift to disgorge them. Just as he was thinking this, the doors opened and he and his father were catapulted out into the stormy night.

They ran all the way home, heedless of the weather. The one was goaded on by irritation; the other was eager to see how the alien called Vateelin might be saved.

CHAPTER 8

Looking After Vateelin

Steven and Jacob worked all through the night. Steven tried to send his son to bed, but Jacob refused point-blank to go.

"I want to see everything. You said I could. And it's Saturday tomorrow; I can sleep late."

"Your mother—" Steven began, but Jacob interrupted him.

"My mother won't even know, unless you tell her," he said. "We've had our supper. She knows you're working—but she'll think I'm already in bed by now."

"Well, sit down," said Steven, "but stay out of the way. I haven't time to argue."

Jacob brought the stool as close as he dared to the desk. He watched as Steven looked into the archives that the Brick—or perhaps one should say "the protection module"—carried under the control of the blue button. His father soon found all he wanted to know about Vateelin.

The script on screen was even smaller than usual. Or maybe Steven had thrown some sort of haze around it. However hard he tried, Jacob could not make out the words. All he knew was that Steven nodded his head from time to time as if it all made sense to him.

Vateelin was, as Steven had suspected, an observer working in isolation, not only from other observers but also from the home planet. He had brought with him his young son, a boy called Tonitheen. Their Earth names were Patrick and Thomas Derwent. What was the purpose of their time on Earth? It was unusual, unheard of, to fetch along a child. It appeared to be some sort of experiment. Thomas Tonitheen, unlike Javayl, had been born on Ormingat and had left there with his father at the age of three. By the time they reached Earth, the child was six years old. Now he would be eleven.

Steven quickly consulted the archive's calendar. The deadline for the Derwents' spaceship to leave Earth was midnight on Saturday, the twenty-sixth of December. Then their ship would leave, with or without its passengers. That was how the system worked. No allowance was made for failure: no failure had ever occurred and so none was ever expected.

"Hard," said Steven musingly to himself. Then, as he thought of where the spaceship was, he sighed and murmured, "Practically impossible. What have I done to deserve this?" For he knew, only too well he knew, that the whole job was his, whether he liked it or not.

He found himself wondering if this experiment had anything to do with his own unheard-of effort—entwining an Earthborn child, of mixed origin, with Ormingat. It would go some way toward explaining why he had never been informed of their presence.

The only other Ormingatrig child Steven knew of was a girl in York whose parents were both from Ormingat. Steven had been notified when she was born. It was a unique event, which had to be entered on his records because it was in his area.

The accident in Casselton, it soon appeared, was in no way caused by any carelessness on Vateelin's part—he had been the victim of a runaway beer tanker whose brakes had failed on a steep hill. It was a horrific thing to happen, and it could have happened to anybody.

"Well," said Jacob impatiently, "are you going to tell me anything?"

Steven paused in his work and told his son all about the accident. It would not do to say too much about Tonitheen, and to mention the girl in York was out of the question.

"Now," he said in conclusion, "we can get on with the real work."

He pushed a yellow button and this produced a map of the North of England. A green button homed in on the very car in Morpeth that had provided Vateelin with a landing place. Then the screen changed from map to picture. Steven could see the car, but wondered if it was at all possible to zoom in enough to find the man he was searching for.

"We'll never find him," said Jacob. "He'll be much too small."

"Be quiet," said his father, frowning.

Working very, very slowly, he zoomed toward the windscreen, and as he got there he perceived a movement, as if some insect were crawling over the bonnet. In further, in further, and there he was, a tiny creature in the shape of a man.

"Wow!" said Jacob. "What is he doing? Where is he going?"

In his hands the tiny man was holding some sort of thread and he was inching toward the side of the bonnet. Steven quickly split the screen so that he could see what was happening in two different dimensions. Then it became clear. Vateelin was trying to lower himself to the ground!

Suddenly he let go of the thread, which did not reach the ground, and went hurtling down into the gutter. Hastily, Steven pushed the scarlet button, the most important button on the Brick. In time to keep breath in the tiny body, but not to save that body from pain, the scarlet button surrounded him with a protective shield. It wafted him away from a grating that could have been the end of him: it would have been impossible to retrieve such a small being from a deep drain.

"See what I saved him from?" said Steven to Jacob. "A split second slower, and our man would have been a goner. It's all skill, you know. Nothing's done by magic. I don't pull rabbits out of hats!"

He looked at Jacob ruefully. "I've got to admit a bit of magic would come in handy right now. We've got to find some way to get that speck all the way to Edinburgh."

"Why Edinburgh?" asked Jacob. "Isn't that miles away from Morpeth?"

"For someone his size, the other side of the road is miles away. But he has to be in Edinburgh because that is where his spaceship is. Bad navigation—even worse than mine. At least our ship is reasonably close to home!"

"So what do we do now?" said Jacob.

"We watch and we study," said Steven, "and we tell ourselves that it *can* be done!"

Vateelin at this point began to make his way to the rear of the car.

"Stay still," snapped Steven, as if the manikin could hear him. "Stay still and let me think, can't you?"

Jacob looked at his father a little dubiously but concluded that he was not talking to him.

Vateelin paused to rest and Steven was relieved. He turned his attention to the Brick itself—to each of its buttons. The gray HELP button seemed the best option. Unfortunately its index did not include instructions on how to return a diminished being to his normal size for the space he is occupying.

Morning came and they were no further forward. During the night, for at least two hours Steven, Jacob, and Vateelin had all slept. Jacob had retired to the armchair when it was clear that there was nothing to see or do.

He woke up with a start and went over to the desk where his father was lying slumped in his chair. "Dad," he said accusingly. "You haven't been watching."

Steven pulled himself back to the upright and said sharply, "If there had been anything to see, I would have seen it."

Then they both turned to the screen.

They gasped at what they saw there. Vateelin was climbing up onto the pavement. Then they saw him jump onto a child's shoe, clinging to the laces. What was he trying to do?

Steven thought rapidly. *In his position, what would I be trying to do?*

Find my way to Edinburgh.

Can't walk all that way.

Go to a station. Get on a train.

Jacob watched. His eyes went from one view to the other. The telemicroscope picture gave an excellent view of Vateelin himself, but was inadequate for any interpretation of his environs. The larger view lost the figure of the man but made it possible to understand just where he was and what he might be trying to do.

Vateelin jumped from the child's shoe and stood at the side of the road. Steven gently maneuvered the equipment to keep him in the center—not easy when Vateelin leapt onto the pedal of a bicycle. Dizzying to watch him as the pedal sped round and round. It stopped. Vateelin jumped off.

Then came a dreadful moment. Jacob grasped his father's shirt-sleeve, bunching it in the palm of his hand. Steven's own hands shook as he furiously directed the shield to envelop his charge.

What had they seen to cause such panic?

There was a dog, a huge lollopy dog, tongue out ready to lick at the patch where Vateelin was standing.

Steven drew breath sharply.

As he paused, Jacob leant right over him and pressed the scarlet button with such force that it screeched.

Vateelin himself must have seen the dog that was menacing him: he suddenly leapt to one side. At that very instant, a nano-second flash of scarlet swept over him and he became the size of an ordinary human being.

"It worked!" said Steven loudly. "God knows how, but it worked!"

It was only after this first reaction that he glared at Jacob. "You had no need to interfere," he said. "I would have managed it myself."

"You weren't fast enough," said Jacob. "Like you said, a split second slower, and he'd have been a goner."

The scarlet button looked slightly lopsided.

"I think you might have broken it," said Steven icily. "I hope it can be mended."

With exaggerated gentleness, he pressed a pink slot and the word REPAIR appeared on the screen. The scarlet button wobbled back to normal, and Steven gave a sigh of relief.

"So what do we do next?" said Jacob.

"Your favorite question!" said Steven wryly, but he gave his son a friendlier look now that the crisis was over. "We do nothing. He'll manage on his own now. He's big enough."

They watched Vateelin walk off down the busy street. They saw people step aside to let him pass. Then they went down to breakfast.

"You work too hard," said Lydia to her husband as she poured out the tea. It did not occur to her that Jacob had been "working" too.

"Only when I have to," said Steven. "Not always. Most of the time, I'm a pretty lazy fellow."

Lydia smiled and shook her head.

It was only much later in the day that Steven thought of the boy, the one who was suffering from shock somewhere. *Where was Patrick/Vateelin's son now? Why have I not been asked to care for him?*

CHAPTER 9

Christmas Eve

For the next few days Steven had no time to think about Vateelin. He learnt from the television and the newspapers that Thomas/Tonitheen was in Casselton General Hospital.

In the meantime, he was busily engaged in updating a computer program for a client of his, an insurance company enthusiastically computerizing risk factors. Steven had no need of subsidies from the purse of Ormingat. There was one brief interruption to his work that week, when Elgarith, the agent in Marseilles, needed protection, but that took no more than an hour of concentrated attention.

Then came Christmas Eve. Lydia took all the children to the vigil mass at St. Joseph's. In the old days it would have been a midnight mass, but times being what they were, it was now celebrated at 8 P.M., after a rousing singsong of all the old-fashioned carols. Beth and Josie loved it and joined in enthusiastically. Jacob sat at the back and stayed silent. The prayers made sense, but he had never been comfortable with all that singing.

While the family were away, Steven turned to the Brick. He had an uneasy feeling that something was happening that was of concern to him. Into the keyboard he instinctively typed the name TONITHEEN.

NO NEED TO KNOW. WE HAVE TRACED THE BOY. HE IS IN CASSELTON GENERAL HOSPITAL.

The words on the screen above the Brick sounded dismissive. That irritated Steven.

"That wasn't hard," he said, flicking the transmit switch that enabled the Brick to receive spoken words. "He has been in Casselton General Hospital since the crash. Don't you have anyone watching terrestrial telly for you? And all the newspapers?"

There was, of course, no spoken answer. The Brick could listen but was not equipped to speak. It was some minutes before fresh words appeared on the screen.

THE VOICE TRACE WORKED. WE HAD NO NEED OF OTHER PATHS.

Then Steven made a mistake he would come to regret, though he did not know it at the moment he made it. He was simply trying to stir things a bit.

"I would have thought that all that publicity would be a worry to those concerned with security! However, I am just the manipulator of one little protection unit. Who am I to criticize a system that has worked for so long?"

The screen cleared, like a self-erasing blackboard.

There was another long pause.

Then more words, ominous words, though Steven did not know it.

WE SHALL GIVE MUCH THOUGHT TO THIS.

At that moment Steven heard the front door opening two floors below. He was about to turn off the Brick, when more words appeared on the screen.

RETURN AT MIDNIGHT. PERMISSION HAS BEEN SOUGHT, BUT NOT YET RECEIVED.

Steven put the Brick in place and gave a sigh. Clearly there was no peace for the wicked! He did not even bother to wonder what this "permission" was all about. He had no doubt he would find out in the wee small hours of the morning.

Downstairs, Lydia and the family had already removed their coats and were going to their rooms to bring down presents for one another, all beautifully wrapped in glossy paper. It had been the custom, ever since the twins had realized that Santa Claus was just a fairy tale, to open all the presents on Christmas Eve and to sleep a little longer next morning. Lydia sometimes missed the whispers and the little voices calling out, "Has he been yet?" whenever she passed the bedroom door. The standard reply was, "No, my loves, he hasn't. He won't come till you're fast asleep!"

After the presents and a little light supper, everyone was supposed to go to bed. Lydia looked surprised when Steven said, "I think I'll wear my new sweater tonight. The computer room can get a bit chilly after the heating goes off. You'd better wear yours too, Jacob. Then we'll not forget it's Christmas."

"Working up there? Tonight?" said Lydia. She had been gathering up the wrapping papers into bundles and putting them into a large plastic bag placed ready on the floor. Pausing in this work was as near as she would come to making any protest.

"Just an idea I want to explore," said Steven soothingly. "And you know how interested Jacob always is."

Lydia stooped to pick up a sheet of glossy green paper. If she was annoyed, she did not show it. "Try not to be too long," she said. "Remember Santa won't come till we're all fast asleep!"

"Ah, but he's been already," said Steven, taking the bundles from her and thrusting them into the bag. "That's where you made your mistake."

He smiled at her fondly as they held the bag between them, shaking all the foil and glitter down into it. The smile asked pardon, and Lydia's returning smile gave it, albeit reluctantly. She shrugged her shoulders and said no more.

*

As soon as the door shut behind them in the computer room, Jacob demanded to know what it was all about.

"Surely they don't want you on Christmas Eve?" he said.

"They do," said Steven, "but I don't know why yet. I suspect it has to do with Vateelin."

Then Jacob forgot that he was a mature fourteen-year-old and said excitedly, "What's happened? Has he shrunk again?"

"I hope not," said Steven. "I can't see that button working for him twice. You nearly broke it the first time."

He set up the Brick on the table, unfurled the screen, and pulled the lever that allowed him to speak to it.

"I am here," he said irritably. "Get on with it."

The Brick answered quite quickly, the words appearing on the screen.

IT IS ELEVEN THIRTY-FIVE, EARTH TIME. PERMISSION HAS NOT YET BEEN RECEIVED.

"Permission for what?" said Steven.

BE PREPARED.

Jacob was sitting on the camp stool by his father's side. He looked at the screen and smiled. "That's not an answer," he said.

"If there is one thing you should have learned by now, my son, it is surely that the machine is stupid when it comes to questions. If the question is the wrong one, or even if it is asked at the wrong time or in the wrong way, no answer will be given."

"Daft," said Jacob.

"And there I absolutely agree with you."

"So what do we do now?"

"We wait till it has something to say to us. Thumb-twiddling time, I think. Or if you care to lie down on the armchair, you can go to sleep till something happens."

So when the machine flickered to life again, Jacob was fast

asleep in the chair, and Steven was once more nodding off at his desk.

PERMISSION HAS BEEN RECEIVED. NOW IS TIME TO INSTRUCT.

Steven was alert immediately. He flicked the switch on the side of the Brick and said, with a yawn, "What time is it?"

TIME IS TO PLAN TO ESCORT VATEELIN. ZOOM IN ON SPACESHIP. EDINBURGH, BY SCOTT MONUMENT.

Wide awake now, Steven manipulated the dials, going from a map of Britain, to the area around Edinburgh, and then into Princes Street, where, at two in the morning, the world was mainly asleep. Jacob woke up at the sound of his father's movements. He came over and joined him just as the map turned into a picture.

The finest probe in the system went down into the soil, then right inside the spaceship, where Vateelin was sleeping uneasily.

At the base of the screen words began to appear, fresh instructions. The picture rolled upward and away, allowing the message to take its place. A larger screen would have been helpful. These instructions were longer than usual.

AT THIS TIME TOMORROW NIGHT, THE SHIP LEAVES EDIN-
BURGH. PERMISSION HAS BEEN GRANTED FOR TRIP TO CASSEL-
TON. PREPARE PATH AND KEEP SHIP UNDER VIGILANCE TILL IT
REACHES CASSELTON GENERAL HOSPITAL. YOU WILL THEN
STRENGTHEN SHIELD AROUND VATEELIN SO THAT HE WILL BE
UNOBSERVED WHEN HE GOES INSIDE THE BUILDING TO FETCH
HIS SON. THEREAFTER, SHIELD WILL EXTEND TO TONITHEEN
ALSO. YOUR DUTIES END WHEN THEIR SHIP LEAVES EARTH.

"Big deal!" said Steven irritably. "Very big deal! It will be the trickiest thing I have ever done. Just think of the variations in size and speed. Some Christmas Day I'll have! I doubt if there'll be time for dinner!"

Jacob gave him a look of encouragement. "You can do it, Dad. You know you can do it. And you'll stop for Christmas dinner because Mum would be hurt if you didn't."

Steven gave a phony yawn. "It's all very well for some," he said. "You be off to bed now. I'd better get started on those beastly calculations."

CHAPTER 10

The Feast of Stephen

Steven appeared for Christmas dinner and joined in quite successfully, though he had allowed himself only two hours' sleep.

"I'll rest tomorrow," he said apologetically to Lydia. "Time zones make it necessary sometimes to work these odd hours, you know that, don't you? I mean—have you any idea what time it is now in Japan?"

"Yesterday," said Lydia, "or, no, I suppose it must be tomorrow!"

He dozed off in his chair till teatime, but straight after tea he left the table and went off to see to more beastly calculations. Jacob made as if to accompany him, but Steven raised his hand and said, "Not this time, Jacob. You would be bored to tears. I know I am!"

Jacob went to bed at his usual time, set his travel alarm to go off at half-past one, and tucked it under his pillow. That way it would be muffled to stop the sound carrying and he would hear it more quickly himself. He fell into so sound a sleep that when it did ring, he did not know what was happening. The clock had found its way to the middle of his bed and was entangled in the sheet.

"Gotcha!" he whispered as he found it and pressed the STOP button. Then he slipped on his dressing gown and went stealthily up the stairs to the computer room.

"Anything happening?" he asked.

"Not yet," said Steven, "but it soon will. Then you'll just have to watch and be completely silent. I've worked everything out, but it will still take concentration."

"Why do they need you?" asked Jacob. "I mean, spaceships land and take off without your help, don't they?"

"They need me," said Steven, "because I know how to control the Brick. And this journey is different and difficult. Most of us who arrive here from Ormingat don't manage to hit our destination spot on—and it doesn't matter: mistakes are allowed for. But in this case, it does matter. That spaceship down there has to land in precisely the right place. The Brick is the only thing that can do that, and it needs careful, calculated manipulation to do it with total accuracy."

They were looking at the split screen again. The larger view showed the base of the Scott Monument, surrounded by scaffolding and protective hoardings. By the law that governs such irritating coincidences, the monument was in the throes of renovation. Vateelin had managed to cope with the problem of reaching his spaceship himself, for which, of course, Steven would give him no credit. The smaller view was a close-up of the inside of the ship, where Vateelin was already putting on his sheepskin coat.

"Why is he doing that?" said Jacob.

"When he reaches Casselton," said Steven, "he will be leaving the ship for a while. It's a cold night. He'll need a coat. That's all."

Vateelin, totally unaware that he was being watched, strapped himself into his seat ready for takeoff.

"Now," said Steven, "not another word."

He stared at the Brick and the screen till he could see nothing else in the room, not even Jacob. Carefully he manipulated the controls. The spaceship shot up out of the soil and hurtled high into the air. Steven sped with it over the hills of southern Scotland, across the border, and down the coast of Northumberland, where the darkness of the night was occasionally interrupted by clusters of light from some small town decked out for Christmas. Within minutes it was in Casselton. Speedily, Steven switched the other view, which for a time had been almost redundant, to the street map of Casselton, homing in on the General Hospital and dragging the spaceship into line to reach it perfectly. It soft-landed in the hospital car park just as one or two heavy flakes of snow began to fall.

"That's the hardest bit done!" said Steven. "What comes next is reasonably simple—more our usual line of business!"

The spaceship disgorged its passenger, rolling him out like a pill. Then he shot up to full size and walked quickly toward the brightly lit doors that led into the Accident and Emergency Department. Steven intensified the shield around Vateelin, making him not truly invisible, but totally unnoticeable.

The doors opened automatically to admit Vateelin and closed again after him. He now knew precisely what he must do. His faith in the shield lay in his own belief that he had produced it himself, of his own strong will. He did not question how he knew exactly where to find his son. He simply walked along the corridors in a direction he believed to be the right one and there, at the end of a long corridor, was the children's ward. Inside the ward, he saw curtains round the bed in the corner nearest the window and he knew at once that his son was there.

For a time, the curtain round the boy's bed interrupted their view. Steven gauged that it was not worth attempting to home in further and surmount this obstacle: they would be out soon enough. Then, as expected, father and son emerged hand in hand and walked quickly out of the ward, along the corridor, through the A&E waiting room, and out into the snowy night.

"Where has he left his coat?" said Steven as he saw that Vateelin was in shirtsleeves. Logic said he must have left it on purpose. And if left on purpose, it must be meant as some sort of message.

"What a stupid, stupid thing to do! Here I am working my guts out to get him safely and inconspicuously away, and he does a daft thing like that!"

Jacob did not need to ask why. They were all, he realized, part of a secret service. Leaving the coat was a clear breach of security.

"You'll have to put that in the report," he said. Jacob by now knew all about Steven's "reports." They had to be made out for every action taken using the protection module. He kept them so brief that from time to time the word ELUCIDATE would flash up on the screen.

Steven grimaced. "I suppose so," he said reluctantly. "Though it might be inviting trouble where none is needed."

He did not know, of course, what trouble his own unguarded remarks to the Cube had already set in motion. He should never have directed attention to Earth's newspaper and television accounts of the crash, no matter how irritated he felt. It would have been much safer to leave the Cube secure in its smugness.

Once outside the building, the lack of a coat clearly made Vateelin shiver.

"Serves him right," said Steven.

Then Jacob saw an ambulance coming down the drive, its headlamps illuminating the flakes of snow. "They're going to get run over," he said anxiously. "That wouldn't serve them right!"

"They've got more sense than that," said Steven. "And if they haven't, there's nothing I can do about it. In fact, I'm worse than useless. That ambulance driver won't even notice them if he mows them down. And it's too late now to withdraw or modify the shield."

So Jacob gave a sigh of relief as he saw Vateelin haul his son back out of harm. After the ambulance had passed them by, in total ignorance of their presence, they crossed to the corner of the car park near the gates where, on the ground, a distinct radiance could be seen against the white of the snow.

"And he'll think that was all his own work!" said Steven. "They all do."

"Have they no powers, then?" said Jacob, thinking not only of Vateelin but of all the other agents he had seen.

"Limited," said Steven. "Some have more than others, but not one of them could really do what the Brick does."

Jacob had thoughts about that boy. Thomas/Tonitheen . . . "He's like me," he said. "A boy with an Ormingat father."

"Not really," said Steven. He was still concentrating closely on the father and son as they went hand in hand toward the spaceship. His answer to his own son was less than thoughtful. "That boy had an Ormingat mother too. He is purebred. He was even born on Ormingat."

Steven did not see his son's eyes glisten. To be described as *purebred* seemed in that instant something very different from *his* situation, and very enviable. *I want to be . . .* , he thought, and did not know how to complete the sentence.

The man and boy shrank into the glow of the ship.

"Thank goodness that's over," said Steven. "I'll get the report done tomorrow, and that, hopefully, will be the end of it."

"You won't forget to tell about the coat," said Jacob.

"I won't forget to tell about the coat," said Steven heavily. "Now get yourself to bed and go to sleep."

Jacob paused a moment at the door, sorely tempted to speak. There was one final thought he was held back from uttering. Would his own father ever return to Ormingat? Who decides who goes home?

CHAPTER 11

Inside Vateelin's Spaceship

The spaceship shot up into the sky above the hospital. The rush to leave Earth's orbit was so great that father and son found themselves clinging to each other on the floor beneath the sofa in the Earth side of the ship.

"We should have been strapped in," gasped Vateelin, holding on tight to Tonitheen and pressing his elbows into the base of the ship in an earnest effort at least to stay in one place till the turbulence was over. "Not long," he breathed, "not long. A few seconds, that's all."

But a few seconds of that force can feel like an eternity. Tonitheen was still an Earth child, and terrified. He dug his fingers into Vateelin's arms and clenched his eyes shut. *Please, God, help us!*

Then a calm came over the ship as it escaped the gravity of Earth. Vateelin and Tonitheen soon found that they were able to sit upright. This was no Earth spaceship. There was no question of floating about once the escape had been made. Each Ormingat ship had its own internal gravity: up was up, and down was down.

They recovered enough to rise from the floor and sit on the sofa. The ship seemed very still.

"We've stopped moving," said Tonitheen anxiously.

"We haven't," said his father. "We are still accelerating, but so smoothly you can't feel it."

Vateelin and Tonitheen, sitting side by side on the long sofa, did not look like parent and child. The slight, slim boy was dark-haired with eyes like jet. His father was fair and well built. Over the next three years, as they journeyed home, they would slowly regain their Ormingatrig features and the Earth genes would be gradually withdrawn. It was a process that had already begun.

"You must be tired, Tonitheen ban. Now it is time for us to sleep."

"Nallytan, Vateelin mesht," said the boy drowsily, automatically using the only Ormingat phrase he really knew. So much had happened, and there had been no time to absorb it all. He curled up in one corner of the sofa.

The lights on the walls of the ship grew dim. Then father and son both slept.

They were awakened when the lights grew bright again, extra bright, and the communication cube glowed spectral green.

Awake, awake, awake! This is emergency. Leave now sleep.

Vateelin opened his eyes and yawned and stretched as if he had been asleep for a week, which is not surprising considering that he had in fact slept for a fortnight.

"What do you want?" he said. "What is it? It can't be time to wake up yet. Otherwise I would feel more rested."

Wake up, Vateelin. Wake up, Tonitheen. Information is required.

Tonitheen stared at the Cube and then tugged at his father's sleeve. Vateelin was still wearing the shirt in which he had entered the ship. It was dry now, and in the warmth of the ship he had long ceased to shiver.

The Cube changed from green to yellow. *It is necessary to discuss your clothing.*

"We needed to become part of the ship again before we could have the energy to refresh ourselves and change," said Vateelin. "You know how swift our departure was. We are still recovering."

It is necessary to make understanding of your lack of coat.

It took Vateelin no more than a second to make sense of this. "I left my coat on the hospital bed," he said. "We of Ormingat have no wish to create difficulties for people on Earth. It was to indicate that my son had not been stolen from the hospital by some stranger."

Sometimes difficulties are unavoidable. You may have betrayed us.

"Besides," added Vateelin thoughtlessly, "I could not go allowing Stella to believe that harm had come to Thomas."

The Cube turned a deeper yellow and began to vibrate.

Say more about Stella. Say more about Stella Dalrymple.

That was a surprise. Of course, Vateelin knew he would have to explain that when he and his son were living on Earth in the village of Belthorp their next-door neighbor, Stella Dalrymple, had become their closest friend, a second mother to Tonitheen, whom she knew as Thomas. The journals Thomas had kept bore Stella's name on nearly every page: these, in microform, would be passed on after they arrived on Ormingat. They had been Tonitheen's work on Earth, written daily and conscientiously from the age of six.

Yet the machine already knew Stella's surname without being told. Where had the information come from? What else did the machine know?

To question would do no good. Vateelin understood the ways of the communicator. So, wearily, he provided some answers.

"Stella Dalrymple was our best friend on Earth for five whole years. She cared for us. She looked after Thomas. She is a widow with no children of her own."

Tonitheen, moved by his father's words, felt tears stinging his eyes. Leaving his beloved Stella had been very, very painful.

"You are upsetting my son," said Vateelin sharply. "To leave the coat was surely a minor infringement."

It is now essential that Ormingat children be removed. Children are danger.

Vateelin did not understand what the machine meant.

Ormingat children? "My son has been removed from Earth. He is here with me now," he said.

There are on Earth two other children of Ormingat entwining. You have made clear the danger of their situation.

This was the first Vateelin had heard of the "other children." He had thought that his son was the only Ormingatrig child ever to visit Earth.

"Who are these children?" he said. "I was told that my son was the youngest ever to leave Ormingat and come to Earth."

No untruth was told. The other children, older than your child, were born on Earth and entwined with Ormingat by their parents. That is why Tonitheen was sent to Earth—to provide control. Now we know that children can betray.

Vateelin thought of the stories his son had told to Stella, of their flight to Earth in a spaceship the size of a golf ball, their diminishing to enter it, and their increasing on leaving it. To allow the child to tell these stories had been a calculated risk.

"No one ever believed him," Vateelin protested. "They simply thought that he had a vivid imagination. No one can accept as truth any story they believe to be completely impossible."

The Cube reverted to its original green.

Not every mind on Earth is completely closed.

"What do you mean?" said Vateelin impatiently.

Stella Dalrymple now believes that the stories your son told her are true. The coat you so carelessly left was matched with a torn strip found on the wheels of the vehicle that nearly killed you. This woman has clearly been able to put the facts together and reach conclusions that should have been beyond her understanding. She should never have believed those stories. Without the mystery of the coat, she never would have done. They were too incredible. You leave us the task of dealing with her.

Tonitheen heard these words and shivered. What did "dealing with her" involve?

"I love Stella," he cried, "and no one must hurt her."

CHAPTER 12

Go to the Spaceship

Steven had not been into the computer room all day.

It was now the eleventh of January and the year had begun so quietly that he could really have no cause for complaint. A routine check each morning and evening did produce the occasional request for help here or there, but nothing startling or urgent. That was the order of things.

And now this! The screen above the Brick had GO TO THE SPACE-SHIP reeling upward and disappearing off the top in obvious agitation. Then it appeared at the foot of the screen, scrolling faster and faster.

"Thought it was too good to last," said Steven. "Whatever it is, I hope it is less frantic than their last effort."

Jacob was downstairs in the sitting room, finishing his homework. He had the room to himself.

"I'm off for a walk," said Steven, looking in at the door as he passed. "How's the homework going?"

Jacob looked up from his book and said hastily, "There's not much left to do. I can finish it off later."

The assumption, of course, was that he would be going to the spaceship. There must have been a summons. Perhaps there would be another adventure. That was Jacob's view—very different from his father's!

A brisk walk through the cool, dark evening brought them to Highgate Cemetery and to their ship once more.

They looked round warily when they reached the Friese-Greene obelisk. Steven did not believe in using a shield for himself unless it had some proper purpose. Self-protection involved extra work and could be a nuisance. All that was required in the quiet of Swains Lane was to be reasonably circumspect.

There wasn't a soul in sight.

Their presence was known to the fox, scrabbling in the soil beneath a nearby angel, digging up a small carcass he had buried there the previous night. Dry twigs and dead branches gave him perfect camouflage. What little noise he made was imperceptible. He paused and froze, ears pricked to listen, his myopic eyes assuring him that the intruders were not in close range. He sniffed the air warily and then, satisfied that there was no immediate danger, returned to his work.

Steven too was content that all was safe. He took out his ruler and unfolded it.

Jacob, as usual, tried very hard to be aware of what was happening as they shrank into the vessel, but, as on other occasions, he could not manage it. First they were outside; then they were inside. And, in between, something was lost.

"Well?" said Steven, addressing the communicator brusquely.

You were expected earlier. There is much to tell.

"We are listening," said Steven, leaving the controls and returning to the sofa, where Jacob was eagerly waiting.

Vateelin made a grave mistake. It will affect all of you.

"Us?" said Steven, not sure who was included in this "all."

You who have children, children of Ormingat.

"In what way?" said Steven sharply. He did not like the sound of this.

Later. First you must understand the gravity. You reported that Vateelin left his torn coat on the hospital bed when he took his son. That was a seriously misguided action on his part.

"Was it?" asked Steven innocently, as if he had attached little importance to this single sentence in his brief report. He was wishing now that he had not put it there at all. He glowered at Jacob, who pretended not to notice.

The communicator did not answer directly, but its next words were revealing.

Now there is a woman of Earth who believes that the boy Tonitheen was telling truth when he told her that he flew there in a spaceship. Before the coat was left, she believed that it was all childish imagination.

"And now?" said Steven.

She has addressed a foolish remark to a reporter.

"Yes?" said Steven tersely.

She gave a cryptic answer to a question. When asked if she could shed light on the disappearance of Vateelin and Tonitheen, she said, "Starlight, perhaps." The reporter was told no more, but that one phrase was enough to set his imagination working. Unfortunately.

Steven nodded, appreciating that the words could just as easily have been ignored. He was about to speak when the Cube resumed, in a tone that could perhaps be interpreted as pompous.

You were right to direct our attention to Earth's newspapers. Copies of all relevant papers have been sent to our agents in York. Their daughter, you remember, was born there.

That statement froze both father and son. Steven was only too aware of the perils that might lie ahead. Jacob was stunned to think that he was not the only young Ormingatriga on this Earth. This was a question he had never thought to ask. He gave his father a look of deep resentment as he realized that this was yet another mind-fenced area. He had come to understand the rules of that particular game. And he did not like it.

Steven weighed up carefully how much he needed to tell Jacob. And, as usual, he wanted to tell him as little as possible. There were many things best left unsaid.

"I'm not happy with all this, *Javayl ban*," he said slowly. He smiled as he pronounced Jacob's special name, but it was a rueful smile.

Jacob was barely listening to him. *These agents in York had a daughter.*

"If they begin to worry about the child in York," Steven went on, "and whether she is likely to betray our secrets, they might decide to recall the whole family. Though I am not at all sure how they would manage it."

"What if they don't want to go?" said Jacob. "They must have lived here a long time. How old is their daughter?"

This line of questioning made Steven feel uncomfortable. Who knew where it might lead?

"She is a year or so younger than you."

"I was born here," said Jacob thoughtfully.

"But she is pure Ormingatrig," said Steven hastily, not wanting his son to guess his own fears. "Bred in the bone, as they say."

Jacob said nothing more. But he thought sadly, *What is bred in my bones? Who am I?* Once again it seemed as if his father were belittling him. *I am less than Ormingatrig. I am also less than human.*

Steven saw the sadness in his son's face and said, "Let's not worry about it yet. We'll see what else the communicator has to say."

He looked toward the silent Cube expectantly.

It glowed white. *Take no more time. Time is important.*

The white glow was a short, sharp warning. Now the Cube turned green again. *The York family will go. You will intervene and correct the mechanism that controls their departure. They will leave Earth on the twenty-fourth of this month. They will be informed of this on the seventeenth. Their entry to the ship should be on the twentieth. That will give sufficient time for proper preparation.*

It was less than three weeks since Vateelin and Tonitheen had made their hasty exit from the planet. It had been hectic and fraught with danger. This was an experience the Ormingatrig would clearly prefer not to repeat.

"*Change the clock?*" said Steven in horror. "That has never, ever been done before. There is no override. I would have thought you would have some other way of recalling agents."

No other way has ever been needed. This is the first premature recall in the whole of our history. You must see to the override. On you we depend.

"It can't be done," Steven repeated. It was one thing to manage the path of a spaceship from one Earth base to another. To change the schedule for a ship's propulsion into orbit was something altogether different.

It will be done. See to it now.

How well they knew Steven! He contradicted, he grumbled, but all the time his mind was working out ways of overriding the clock.

Go.

There was a shiver of air in the ship as the door divided. Steven and Jacob were drawn toward it. They had been dismissed.

As they walked back home, Jacob's first question was, thankfully, an easy one.

"What clock is it that you have to change?" he said.

"There is a clock in the base of every ship—remember the clock in ours? Each clock is set to its own time. For a ship to return to Ormingat, its time must be fixed at the outset—the globules fall into place along the arrow, and when they are all in line, a firing takes place that is more or less like the action of a rocket in one of Earth's spaceships, but much more concentrated."

"So is our clock set too?" asked Jacob, the thought taking shape before Steven had time to fence it. "Then you will have to go? And what about me?"

"It's set for years from now," said his father with a conviction he did not really feel. "We don't even need to think about it."

They walked on for a while in silence.

"And will you be able to alter the clock in York?" said Jacob. He looked at his own watch. It was ten minutes to eight.

"I might," said Steven, looking sour. "I probably will. But why can't they let me alone? I am supposed to deflect attention. I do that remarkably well."

"You do everything well, Dad," said Jacob.

"I probably do," said Steven as if stating a simple fact. "More's the pity! A willing horse gets all the work."

Jacob laughed, releasing nervous energy. "I'd hardly call you that!" he said.

"It depends on what you mean by willing," said Steven, grinning. "I didn't say I was happy about it!"

CHAPTER 13

A Monumental Mistake

Late that night, after the rest of the family were in bed asleep, Jacob went to the computer room to find his father already seated before the Brick, calling up the map of York. Silently he sat on the stool beside him.

Onto the screen above the Brick came the outline of the minster, casting a shadow over the street map. Steven manipulated the keys on the Brick till the image moved to the north, to the houses in Linden Drive, to the back garden of number 8, and then—Jacob gasped as he saw it—right to the bulbous eyes of an enormous stone frog.

"There," said Steven, holding the image and sitting back for a moment to contemplate.

"What now?" said Jacob.

"Now," said Steven ruefully, "I must get a probe to penetrate right through that monster so that I can see inside their spaceship and tamper with the clock. Heaven alone knows if I'll be able to manage it."

At that moment he was concentrating his mind on how the clock, with no override, could be changed. He did not realize that there was another serious obstacle to be overcome before he could begin.

He leant forward to the Brick and began skillfully to create a laserlike probe and direct it very precisely at the center of the frog's head, between those two protruding eyes.

Then . . . Go!

Then . . . Go! Go!

But the probe went no further than the surface of the frog.

Steven increased the power as far as he could.

Go! Go! Go!

He sat back and exhaled loudly.

"What's wrong?" said Jacob.

"I'll tell you what's wrong," said his father crossly. "That big, ugly monstrosity of a beast squatting in that little pond's what's wrong!"

Jacob stared at the screen where the frog sat immutable, surrounded by a narrow moat of water.

Steven sighed.

"It seemed such a good idea at the time, a good place to conceal the spaceship. Mind you, I remember thinking, 'They've got a hope!' Do you know how many times a ship lands spot on target? No more than twice in a hundred years! And here we were hoping that this one would set down plumb in the middle of a little pond behind a very ordinary suburban house in York!"

"But what about the frog, Dad?" asked Jacob, trying to make sense of what was being said.

"The frog was already there in the back garden. The previous owner of the house was a sculptor with crazy ideas about size. That was something we clearly sympathized with! Our people acquired it, complete with frog, and thought what a good housing the pond would make for our craft. So the pond was drained and the frog was rolled back onto the lawn, ready for the ship to land, spot in the center like an arrow hitting a target. From all that distance! I remember thinking it was laughable. But it made it. I was really thrilled when it did—and not just because it saved me the job of guiding its passengers to their new home and checking that the landing site was viable."

"You watched them arrive?" said Jacob, encouraging his father to tell more.

"I watched it. You were still a baby and the twins hadn't been thought of yet. I even remember when their child was born, a little girl they called Nesta—Neshayla at her entwining. She's a year younger than you. It was a totally unexpected event, as you can imagine, but there was no problem with her entwining, both parents being Ormingatrig."

Jacob winced, but Steven did not notice it.

"A smug little family, I always thought," he went on. "Sitting pretty in that house in York, doing their bit of research, reporting home once a year with all their findings. Nice work if you can get it, as the saying goes. And here am I slogging away year after year, keeping them all out of trouble. Then there are observers like Elgarith who have to live by their wits from day to day and need constant watching. The Gwynns don't know they're born!"

But now Steven had had his pause. He bent over the Brick again and made one more futile effort to penetrate the skull of the frog.

"It just can't be done," he said, sitting back and looking at Jacob almost hopefully, as if his son could come up with an answer. "Clearly situating the ship beneath that—that object was a monumental mistake."

Jacob suppressed a grin at his father's unwitting pun. "Can you not move the frog somehow?" he said. "I mean push it to one side for the probe to enter?"

"Telekinesis?" said his father. "Not a hope. The Brick is fine-tuned, a subtle object, not designed to work by brute force. Kraylin had the earthmover—the Super Telekinesis Instrument—but it broke down five years ago, just before Kraylin was due to return to Ormingat. He has never been replaced—and neither has the STI!"

Father and son looked blankly at the screen as if trying to outstare the frog.

"There is one way," said Steven meditatively. "If I could go up there, trowel out a small hole, and insert a tube diagonally into the soil outside the pond, the ship would soon draw it in to make contact as soon as it identified its source. We are incredibly clever, you know, even if we aren't perfect!"

"So you'll go to York tomorrow?" said Jacob. "Can I come with you?"

"It's not as simple as that," said Steven. "I can't be in two places at once, and if it is going to work, I have to be here to manage the Brick."

"I could do that," said Jacob. "At least I think I could."

"You couldn't, *Javayl ban*," said Steven, "not to the level that is needed. It is not just a matter of pressing a few buttons."

He bit his lip as he pondered his next suggestion.

"You could go to York," he said. "I would watch you every step of the way and my protection would be all around you. Nothing could go wrong. Nothing could possibly harm you."

"What if it draws me in? Our ship does. Will I be able to get out again?"

Steven smiled. "Nothing more simple," he said. "It's my job, after all! You shall be totally protected, even from the Gwynn spaceship. It will draw in the probe, just far enough, nothing else. I shall be completely in control."

Then Jacob thought of another, more mundane problem. "Tomorrow's Tuesday," he said. "I have to go to school. What would Mum say?"

"I'll see to that," said Steven eagerly. "Don't worry. I'll see to everything."

At breakfast, after the twins had gone to catch their bus, Steven said to Lydia, "Jacob won't be going to school today."

Jacob, at a nod from his father, got up and left the room.

"Well," said Lydia calmly, "and what is Jacob doing today?"

"He is going to help me. This afternoon he has to go to York on an errand for me. I know it's unusual and that he ought to be in school, but I think we can waive the rules for once in a while, don't you?" He smiled at Lydia, the buccaneer smile.

Lydia looked doubtful. "It seems an odd thing to do," she said, "at such short notice."

Steven took her hand in his. Their eyes met in what could have passed for frankness.

"It's to do with my work," he said softly. "I need Jacob to be in a place some miles away to test communications on my latest system. He'll be perfectly safe. He's fourteen and he is clever and resourceful. So let's give him the chance. He'll be home again early this evening. It's really no more than a flying visit. And he knows exactly what he has to do."

"Is there nothing I can do?" said Lydia. "Should I go with him?"

"He'd be insulted," said Steven, looking appalled. "He'd think you thought he couldn't manage on his own. And we both know that he can."

Lydia had to agree but she looked disappointed: she would not have minded joining in the trip to York! The twins were at school and Steven's presence made sure that they would not be returning to an empty house.

Steven saw her faltering and said sweetly, "You can run him to the station if you like. That would be a real help."

CHAPTER 14

Jacob in York

Lydia took her son to King's Cross. It was a cold morning. While they waited for the train, she took Jacob into the snack bar, where they had a pot of tea—"to warm you up." It was not her way to fuss, but she was pleased when Jacob zipped up his jacket and put on his woolen gloves as they went out onto the platform. He had no case with him, just the sports bag he usually took to school. It did not look very full or very heavy. Presumably there was equipment inside for whatever experiment it was they were engaged in.

"Take care," she said as he boarded the train. "And get home as quickly as you can."

In the car she had asked no questions about Jacob's errand. He had volunteered the information that his father wanted him in York for something to do with "transmission." It made it sound as if Steven were engaged in some scientific experiment, like a latter-day Marconi or Logie Baird.

"As soon as I've made contact, I just come back home," said Jacob. "It's not much of a job really."

Why York?

Why anywhere? York made as much sense as any other location would have done. They must be using a vantage point there, she supposed. The minster? Clifford's Tower? Lydia made a point of not being inquisitive. The whole family had been to the city just two years ago on a visit to the Jorvik Centre. So to choose York for this experiment was not so very strange.

Just after four o'clock, Jacob got off the bus at the corner of Linden Drive in a suburban estate to the north of York. It had not been difficult to get there: his father's directions were very precise, down to a graphic description of the bus route from the stop outside the station to the stop nearest the home of the Gwynn family.

It was dusk on a dull afternoon. The dark would not be long in coming. For Jacob, of course, neither the dark nor the light was unsafe. No one would observe him, night or day. No one would molest him, whether to rob or to terrorize. The shield about him left him visible but unnoticed. In London, his father was watching him every step of the way on the screen above the Brick.

Two people, clearly mother and daughter, got off the bus at the same stop as he did. Jacob found himself following them into Linden Drive and overhearing their conversation. They sounded faintly American.

"Is it all right if I go shopping with Amy on Saturday?" said the girl. "She needs a new pair of hockey boots."

"Sure," said her mother. "Only don't stop out too late. It gets dark so early. And you never know who's prowling about these days."

"Oh, Mom!" said the girl. "Do you think I can't take care of myself?"

For some reason that neither Jacob nor the girl could appreciate, that remark made the mother put an arm round her daughter's shoulder and give her a hug.

Overprotected, thought Jacob. Then another, rueful thought came to him. He grinned self-mockingly. *But not as overprotected as I am! Nobody could be!*

The couple reached the gateway to number 8 and went in. It was only then that Jacob knew they were the Gwynns. He shivered as he realized that there were things he knew about their destiny that they could not even suspect. Jacob was here on their home territory to do a job that would take the Gwynn family right out of this solar system within a matter of days. Perhaps the mother sensed something; maybe that was why she had given her daughter that impulsive hug.

Jacob dawdled till the Gwynns had gone into the house and shut the door behind them. Theoretically, he could have followed them into the drive, even into the house, and they would have ignored him. But it seemed prudent not to push protection too far.

After the Gwynns were out of sight, there was no one else in the street either to notice or not to notice him. It was beginning to rain, a cold, misty drizzle. Jacob opened the gate, went in, and closed it behind him. He took the path to the side of the house, which was skirted by a high, thick hedge that separated the Gwynns' garden from the one next door. When he reached the back garden, the first thing he saw was the frog, sitting there, squat and monstrous on its lily pad in a disproportionately small pond.

He went up close to it and sat down on the grass, taking his bag from his shoulder and unzipping it.

From the bag he took out three pieces of equipment, none of them extraterrestrial, all very common. There was a telescopic tube, "borrowed" from the handle of the carpet sweeper; a small trowel; and his father's mobile phone.

"Dad," said Jacob into the phone that he was not normally allowed to use (the Bradwells were not keen on their children using mobiles), "I'm here in the back garden."

"I see you, Son," said Steven. "You have nothing to worry about. Don't use the phone again till I ring you. Now do exactly as we arranged."

Jacob stood up and circled the pond, gauging the direction till he was sure he was on the southern side of it. Then he squatted down and with the trowel he made an indentation in the soil. It was hardly big enough for a game of marbles. The ground was hard. The rain was now falling more heavily on Jacob's head and shoulders. He found himself wishing, grumpily—like father like son!—that the shield could offer protection against the weather.

The mobile went: *Diddley-dom. Diddley-dom.*

There was a text message: USE YOUR FINGERS.

Jacob looked down at his gloves doubtfully and then, with reluctance, began to push crumbs of soil out of the hole he was trying to make. The gloves were soon soggy and the hole was not much bigger.

Diddley-dom. Diddley-dom.

Another text message: TAKE YOUR GLOVES OFF. USE YOUR FINGERNAILS.

Thank you, Dad, said Jacob inside his head. *Thank you very much.*

He glared in the direction he had established as south, removed the gloves, and, distastefully, dug his nails into the ground. The area he could cover this way was clearly limited, but within this area he made progress. A hole the size of three fingers was dug down to a depth of six inches, give or take a centimeter.

Biddley, biddley, biddley. Biddley, biddley, bi-id—

Jacob took the mobile from his pocket again and put it to his ear.

"You're doing fine," said his father's voice. "Couldn't have done better myself. Now all you need to do is pull out the rod, probe it into the hole you've made, and bang hard on it with the trowel. I wish I'd thought to give you a hammer."

Jacob did not deign to reply. He doggedly assembled the sweeper handle, pushed it into the hole, and banged vigorously on the end of it. The noise of clashing metal on metal should have drawn the attention of the lady in the house next door to the Gwynns', who was making one of her regular surveys of the territory. But Mrs. Jolly was totally unaware of Jacob. The shield was truly a powerful force.

Then, wonder of wonders, the hammering worked. The probe began to enter the soil. Just an inch or two at a time, or maybe a couple of centimeters. Then, *whoosh!* contact was established with the ship itself and it anxiously swallowed the whole handle till only a small shoot was left visible above-ground.

I hope I can get it out again, thought Jacob. *Mum is sure to want to know where her sweeper handle's gone!*

CHAPTER 15

Jacob's Decision

Back in the computer room, Steven whistled his relief. He saw the probe sucked into the soil and then bent eagerly over his keyboard. Visible on the screen above the Brick was the hollow end of the sweeper rod projecting out of the ground. Gently steering, Steven made the beam enter its shaft and go down, down, down, until he had a view of the interior of the Gwynns' spaceship. That was still not close enough. He did not need to see their living quarters, their laboratory, or even the cuboid communicator. He maneuvered and manipulated till he had a view of the inner workings of the clock. It filled the screen with the image of artificial stars in a swirling galaxy.

This, he thought, *will take hours, maybe days. I can't leave Jacob there in the garden much longer. He will have to come home.*

"And leave the sweeper handle here in the garden?" said Jacob, aghast, when his father spoke to him again on the mobile. "I can't do that. Mum needs it. She'll want to know where it is. Try hard, Dad. I'll wait here till I can pull it out and fetch it home with me."

"It doesn't matter," said Steven impatiently. "I'll tell your mother a story. I'll tell her I broke it. I'll buy her another one. Come on, Jacob. Get out of there and catch the bus back to the station. It is already five-fifteen. Your mother will be more worried about you being late than about a sweeper handle. You must know that."

"Give it another hour, Dad," said Jacob. "I don't know what you told Mum about me coming here, but tell her not to worry and that I'll be on the seven o'clock train. Changing a clock shouldn't take that long, surely?"

Jacob switched off.

A text message from Steven said curtly: COME HOME, NOW.

Jacob's reply said equally curtly: LET ME KNOW WHEN I CAN PULL THE HANDLE OUT OF THE SOIL.

Steven gave a sigh and turned to the job in hand. He could not spend any longer arguing with a bolshie teenager. He had never thought of Jacob in that light before, but now thoughts that encompassed *I don't know where he gets it from* rumbled through his mind!

Jacob was standing in the rain with dirty hands, suffering a measure of discomfort that would have made a warm bus and a comfortable train really attractive. But he had decided that he wanted to spend more time around this house. He wanted to see its occupants, especially the girl who was fully Ormingatrig but had been born here on Earth.

He knew that his father would no longer be actively watching him. The shield would remain, but Steven would be busy adjusting the space clock.

Jacob wiped his hands on his coat and made his way toward the house. There was a back porch where he could shelter from the rain, but he was not interested in that. What he wanted was a window he could look through. On this side of the house the curtains were closed. Chinks of light showed through the kitchen window, but there was no chance of seeing inside. Jacob walked round to the front and was rewarded with the sight of a window where the light was on but no one had yet bothered to draw the curtains.

The girl was there—a slightly built girl with mousy hair, sitting curled up on the sofa talking to a cat and stroking the fur between its ears. A year younger than himself? Yes, possibly. So this was Nesta. Had she been told where her parents came from?

As he watched her, it seemed to him that she was prettier than he had thought at first glance; quietly and peacefully pretty. She also looked vulnerable: the thick jumper she was wearing was about two sizes too big, which probably made her look slighter than she actually was. Seeing her, and knowing a little of what the future held for her, Jacob felt concerned. How much did she know? How would she cope with the journey to Ormingat? He had already heard her telling her mother her plans for Saturday: but by then the family would have been told the devastating news. What would her friend's hockey boots matter then?

Suddenly, Nesta got up and the cat tumbled off her knee, complaining briefly before digging its paws into the side of the sofa.

"Charlie," said Nesta, loudly enough to be heard by Jacob, who was standing with his forehead pressed against the glass. "You know you're not supposed to do that."

She then walked right up to the window and raised her hands to close the curtains. She was standing right in front of him. He gazed at her. She looked out into his eyes. For no more than a split second the shield failed, and then it was intact again. But Nesta felt the hairs on the back of her neck prickle. It was too brief a glimpse to be assimilated. It was no more than a shiver, as if someone had walked over her grave. Hastily she finished closing the curtains.

Jacob's heart leapt with the awareness that she had noticed him. "Nesta," he whispered. He rested hands and head against the pane of glass. After many minutes, a noise in the garden disturbed him. He turned away from the darkened window and was caught in the headlamps of a car turning into the drive. The lights dazzled him, but the man in the car saw nothing of the figure in front of him. Jacob stood to one side and watched the driver put the car away before going into the house. This must be Nesta's father.

Jacob returned to the back garden and stood in the shelter of the porch. He waited with the mobile in his hand, hoping his father would ring to say all was ready. The rain rattled on the roof. Jacob was so miserably cold that he could last out no longer. He used the mobile again.

"I think I should come home now, Dad," he said. "You're right. We can buy another carpet sweeper for Mum."

"It's okay," said Steven with a yawn. "I was just about to ring you. You can bring the handle back. I've done better than I thought. All it took was concentration."

"I might not be able to get the handle out of the ground," Jacob confessed. "There's not much of it left above the surface."

"Put on your gloves again," said his father. "Push your forefinger into the top of the handle, then heave. My guess is that the ship will release it when it feels you pulling. They know what I have done. They know I have no further need of it."

Jacob did as he was told and found himself sitting heavily on the grass as the handle flew out at an unexpectedly high speed. When he recovered, he collapsed the handle into its four small parts and placed it in his sports bag beside the trowel.

The home journey was straightforward. It was his father who met him at King's Cross. Jacob was still muddy and his hands were grazed.

"Nice work," said Steven, barely noticing the mess his son was in.

"I suppose you could call it that," said Jacob sourly, employing his father's usual turn of phrase. "I'll be happier when I'm home and out of this wet coat."

CHAPTER 16

What Next?

"So what happens next?" asked Jacob on Wednesday evening as they sat once more in the computer room.

Steven was puzzled for an instant. Life had contained a whole day of varied activity. The observer in Marseilles had needed attention yet again—a minor problem but quite time-consuming; the insurance company had phoned twice about their digitization; the twins had needed help with their math homework; and dinner had been an exceptionally nice spaghetti Bolognese.

"Happens next?" he said. "Oh—in York, d'you mean?"

"Yes, Dad, where else?"

"I don't know," said Steven. "At least, I don't know what is happening now or will happen in the next few days. It is no concern of mine. A week come Saturday I shall, purely as a matter of interest, set the observation module ready to watch the Gwynns' departure and, as it were, to close the book on it."

"Like we did with Vateelin and Tonitheen?"

Steven smiled, proud of his son's ability to remember and pronounce the names so correctly. "You might be Ormingat born and bred to hear you, *Javayl ban*," he said affectionately.

"But I'm not, am I?" said Jacob in a sharp tone that his father failed to understand. *I want to be one thing*, he thought bitterly, *not a mixture.*

"What will they think about returning to Ormingat?" he went

on, before his father could think of any follow on to the rhetorical question. "I mean, will they want to go?"

"Yes," said Steven, weighing his words carefully. "Any of us without ties on Earth would be delighted to leave early. Earth duty is interesting and important, but—and I know you won't understand this—it is somehow divorced from reality. For Ormingatrig, Ormingat is always the real world."

"What about Nesta?" said Jacob harshly. "She was born here in this second-class world."

"I didn't say that," said Steven hastily. "Earth is not second class. It is just different, and some of the differences are not good. You should know that. God forbid that I should not know how lucky I am. To be married to your mother is a privilege. To be father to such a wonderful Earth family makes up for any sense of loss. That's what I mean about 'ties on Earth.'"

"But what about Nesta?" persisted Jacob. He remembered so well the girl he had seen through the window. He had looked into her eyes, and for just a moment she, he was sure, had looked into his. In that brief second she had noticed him, and he was oh so used to being unnoticed.

"She will know of her Ormingat lineage. She will have learnt of it gradually from infancy. She too will be ready and eager to leave," said Steven.

"I learnt nothing of my Ormingat lineage, as you call it, till I was thirteen," said Jacob. "How do you know that her parents don't have as little sense as you did in this matter?"

"That," said Steven indignantly, "is a completely different situation. You are Lydia's son as well as mine."

There it rested for another couple of days. But Jacob brooded on it and kept seeing the eyes of the girl at the window. He longed to see her again and to know if she would show any sign of recognition. It was a tantalizing thought.

On Friday afternoon he came home from school and went straight to the computer room, where Steven was engaged in producing some complicated graph on his ordinary Earth computer.

"One minute," he said, not looking away from the screen. "Just got to work this out."

Jacob sat down on the stool and waited impatiently.

"Well," said Steven at last, "what is it?"

"I think we should check on the family in York," said Jacob. "I have a hunch that something could go wrong. I've been thinking about it all day."

Steven sighed. "Waste of time," he said. "Nothing can go wrong. Matthew knows what he's doing. He and Alison need no further help from me. They have never needed my help in all the time they have been here."

"Look anyway," said Jacob, "just to satisfy me."

Steven moved over to the Brick, drew out its keyboard, and unfurled its screen.

"Just a short look," he said, "but I'm telling you now, all we'll see is a twilit garden and that ugly great frog. I can't and won't probe inside the house. It is none of my business. It is against all etiquette, if you understand what I mean."

What they saw was not what Steven had expected. For a start, the twilit garden was partly illuminated by the porch light. Coming out of the porch were Nesta and her mother; Matthew was ahead of them. Then all three surrounded the frog in the pond.

"They're moving the frog," whispered Jacob, almost as if he feared they might hear him.

"They must have to enter the ship for some reason," said Steven, "although this is a few days earlier than I would have expected."

Then it became clearer to him. They were not all entering the ship. Just one. Just Matthew. With breathtaking speed he disappeared into the center of the pond—he simply vanished.

Jacob had seen this sort of thing happen before: with Vateelin and his son outside the hospital. He had experienced it himself several times in the cemetery at Highgate. But the wonder of it never decreased. On this occasion, the event was so unexpected that Jacob blinked hard. His eyelids clenched out the scene just long enough for him to miss Nesta's startling reaction.

"She's collapsed," cried Steven in alarm. "She's gone into a dead faint."

Jacob jumped. He looked at the screen and saw that Nesta's mother was struggling to support her daughter and was half carrying her toward the house.

"What a stupid way to let her know!" said Steven in anger.

"What do you mean, Dad?" said Jacob anxiously. He wanted to follow Nesta into the house. He wanted to know that she was recovering.

"I'll tell you what I mean," said Steven angrily. "Those two paragons in York have failed to tell their daughter anything till now. And they have demonstrated diminishing to a total innocent."

"You demonstrated diminishing to me," said Jacob resentfully. "So what's the difference?"

"I guided you through the experience," said Steven self-righteously. "I didn't just diminish before your eyes and leave you to stand watching. It was utter folly. I don't envy them the next few hours."

"So what happens next?" said Jacob for the second time that week.

"I don't know," said Steven tersely. "I don't care. And it's not my job. Let them get on with it."

As he spoke, he made the screen go dead and furled it back into the Brick.

CHAPTER 17

The Next Day

"It's getting stuck in an infinite loop," said Steven patiently. "That's because you've forgotten to increment the counter."

The program was failing to respond and Jacob didn't know what to do next.

They had been working on the computer for about an hour—the Earth computer, that is. Steven was teaching his son some programming of a rather more complex nature than that offered by the school curriculum.

Jacob was undeniably interested in these computing lessons, but today he was finding it difficult to concentrate. His attention kept straying to the Brick on the desk, hoping that a message would appear on-screen or that the purple button would begin to flash. But nothing happened.

Steven leant over him and added the missing instruction. The program was successfully restarted. "There," he said. "That fixes it."

Jacob was paying little attention. His mind was definitely elsewhere. He tried hard to turn his thoughts to the work in hand. But it was no use. He could hold back no longer.

"Can we look in on York again, Dad?" he said. "To see how they are doing, to check how Nesta is?"

"No," said his father. "We can't. We are not here as spectators.

We watch only when required, and we watch only what we are meant to see. It is not a game."

"We looked yesterday, without any summons," said Jacob.

"There are rules," said Steven loftily. "I do break them occasionally, but that doesn't mean I don't respect them. Yesterday was, I know now, a mistake."

"So when do we next watch what happens there?" said Jacob.

"Unless I hear to the contrary," said Steven, "I shall be watching out for the departure of their ship one week today. It is scheduled to leave at two A.M. on Sunday the twenty-fourth. I shall settle down to inspect sometime before midnight on Saturday. It will be a tedious couple of hours, no doubt, but we are meant to err on the side of safety."

This was news to Jacob. He had assumed the work was finished and that all they would be doing was watching that 2 A.M. take-off. What safety was his father talking about?

"Something could go wrong?" asked Jacob anxiously.

"Unlikely," said his father. "Ninety-nine point nine percent unlikely. But we shall watch, nevertheless."

"If anything did go wrong, could you help?" said Jacob. He thought anxiously about Nesta needing to be rescued from a ship running out of control.

"Nothing will go wrong," said Steven adamantly.

"But if it did?"

"It would have to go in my report," said his father irritably. "How much power do you think we have?"

Steven did not tell Jacob about the call he had the following Thursday, late at night. He had been filing a report on an action in Oxford where his intervention had been necessary—and successful. Suddenly, just as he was thinking of retiring for the night, the purple button began to flash. On screen came the words:

NESTA HAS DISAPPEARED.

That was all. Steven gave a yawn and slipped the lever that permitted speech.

"What do you mean? Disappeared?"

In his tired state, he was thinking that Nesta had somehow shrunk "out of context." He found himself hoping that it would not all turn too complicated, especially if it should involve an immediate visit to the spaceship. He didn't relish the thought of trekking up Swains Lane so late at night in weather that was far from clement.

NESTA'S PARENTS ARE UNABLE TO FIND HER.

"Why can't they find her?" said Steven. "She's probably hiding somewhere. Kids are like that. They think it's fun. Tell them to check the cupboard under the stairs. That's a favorite place."

SHE HAS LEFT A MESSAGE. SHE HAS RUN AWAY.

"That's serious," said Steven more soberly, "but it doesn't sound like work for me. I have never been asked to deal with a runaway before. I wouldn't know where to begin."

DO WHATEVER YOU CAN.

Steven sighed. He made a fruitless attempt to set up some sort of trace on her. He knew from the start that it would be futile. Nesta did not want to be found and no one knew where she had gone. Even terrestrial sources gave no clues at all. Compared with this search, finding Vateelin on the bonnet of that car in Morpeth had been a piece of cake.

"It can't be done!" he said angrily to the screen, after he had played around with the controls for over an hour. There was simply nothing to go by, nothing to hold on to.

IT CAN'T BE DONE.

"That's what I've just said."

NOT ENOUGH DATA.

"Precisely. And the girl does not want to be found."

THE GIRL DOES NOT WANT TO BE FOUND.

Steven drew a breath of frustration. The communicator was being even more obtuse than usual.

"And if she does not return in time," said Steven firmly, "then the Gwynns must return without her. The clock cannot be reset again."

PRECISELY.

In the days that followed, Steven avoided talking about the Gwynns. Whenever Jacob mentioned them, he took evasive measures and changed the subject. If his son was so concerned about the well-being of that girl in York, it would be cruel to tell him that Nesta had run away from home rather than face the journey to Ormingat.

CHAPTER 18

Spies

The village of Belthorp, where Thomas and his father had lived for five years, had been the focus of attention at the time of their disappearance. But, for now, things were settling back to normal. On the Saturday after Nesta's disappearance, life there was going on as usual.

In the flat above the newsagent's shop, which was also the proprietor's family home, Mrs. Swanson stood glaring at her two sons, the elder of whom had just smashed the training tower his younger brother had spent the last half hour building up. A bivouac tent had collapsed in the middle of the floor and half a dozen Action Men were impeding access to the window.

"This room looks as if a bomb's hit it!" said Mrs. Swanson. "Get those toys cleared away—and close the curtains before you put the light on. If everything's not back in place by the time I come up here again, there'll be no video and no pizza for you two tonight."

Videos were a Saturday evening treat, together with pizzas delivered to the door in their boxes.

Philip shrugged, as if he didn't care. At eleven, he was a shade more defiant than his younger brother. "Don't look at me," he said. "Most of that mess is his, not mine."

"But you made it," said Anthony, stifling a yawn. "It was you knocked the training tower down."

"You told me to dive-bomb it!" said Philip, outraged. "You can't dive-bomb it without knocking it down!"

"Look," said their mother, "I don't care who did what. I want this place tidied up."

"Tidyin' up's women's work," said Anthony in a sleepy voice. He was echoing words he had heard others say, without paying much attention to their meaning. He was just nine and small for his age, not robust like his brother. He usually went to sleep well before the end of any video.

"And untidying is man's work?" said his mother dryly as she picked up a pajama top and threw it in his direction. "Don't try to be clever. It doesn't suit you. Just get on with the job. And don't leave it all to Philip!" With those words, she went out and closed the door behind her.

Immediately, the two were friends again, for a while anyway.

"Let's just put the light on," said Philip, "and not draw the curtains. I don't know why she's so fussy. Nobody can see in, unless they're in a low-flying airplane!"

"Or on a double-decker bus maybe?"

"Double-decker buses don't come here," said Philip as he languidly pulled the toy box to the middle of the floor and began throwing things into it just any old how.

"That's not the way to do it," Anthony protested.

"If you want it done any better," snapped Philip, "you can do it all yourself."

Anthony reddened and looked close to tears.

"Come on," said Philip, "we'll not fight about it. Tell you what—let's play spies first."

Anthony brightened. "We'll watch for the woman from the Grange," he said.

"Too soon for that," said Philip. The woman from the Grange

walked her Alsatians round midnight. The boys had already spied on her two or three times and identified her as the leader of a witches' coven.

"So who'll we spy on?" said Anthony.

"We'll watch for who gets off the next bus. There's bound to be some suspicious characters."

"Like Mrs. Bigwood?" said Anthony.

"Nah—stupid! Mrs. Bigwood only wears funny hats. We'll look for strangers wrapped up in mufflers or wearing balaclavas."

Philip switched off the light again.

They both went to the windowsill and picked up the binoculars they'd each been given for Christmas. They weren't high-precision instruments, but they were adequate for bird-watching on a modest scale, and looking at unsuspecting people passing along the street.

The bus came. At the stop at the end of Merrivale, five passengers alighted.

"There's Mrs. Bigwood!" said Anthony excitedly. "And she's got her umbrella hat on again!"

Philip did not deign to answer him. The bus went onward to the stop beside the Green. He trained his binoculars on it and Anthony followed suit. The bus carried on out of the village, leaving just two more passengers standing in its wake.

"There's a man with a muffler," said Anthony, nudging his brother's arm. "A tall man with a long overcoat. He looks like a Russian."

"Rubbish!" said Philip loftily. "That's Nico Montori's dad. He always wears that scarf."

Anthony was resigned to spying failure when Philip said, "But you have missed the obvious. What about the girl who got off the bus at the same time?"

At that moment, Mr. Montori could be seen speaking to this other passenger. Then he waved both arms and walked briskly away from her. She looked round as if puzzled. Then she sat on Councillor Philbin's park bench. Her back was to the boys, but they both saw her bend forward as if crushed by some great problem.

"I've never seen her before," said Philip. "Now that's a real mystery."

"There's Mickey Trent," said Anthony, looking further up the road toward the church. "I bet he's been to his auntie Fay's."

"He's stopping," said Philip, adjusting the binoculars to get the best possible view. "He's talking to the girl."

The girl stood up and she and Mickey walked across the Green toward Merrivale. They went in through the gate of number 12. Mrs. Dalrymple opened the door to them. Then Mickey walked quickly away and the girl went inside the house.

"She's gone into Mrs. Dalrymple's," said Philip. "Now what can that be about? Maybe she knows something. Maybe she's found Thomas Derwent!"

The disappearance of Thomas and his dad was the biggest mystery the village had ever known. It definitely gave inspiration to young sleuths, constantly looking to find something that their elders and betters had missed.

The bedroom door opened and Mrs. Swanson switched on the light.

"That's it," she cried, stomping over to the window to close the curtains. "You'll tidy this place within the next half hour and then you'll go straight to bed. I might as well talk to myself as try to tell you two to do anything!"

"But there's a strange girl gone into Mrs. Dalrymple's," said Philip, anxious to calm his mother down and distract her attention. "Mickey Trent took her there. And we've never seen her before."

But Mrs. Swanson would not be placated or diverted. "Tidy up," she said shortly, "and then bed. I don't want to hear anything about anybody. Understood?"

"Yes, Mam," said both boys together.

*

The girl who had just entered number 12 Merrivale was Nesta Gwynn, the runaway from York. For the past three nights she had stayed in the garage at the back of her friend Amy's house. Amy had made a great job of hiding her, but she couldn't stay there on Saturday because Amy's brother would be home from college and he used the garage for his motorbike. So Nesta had taken the train north and was resolved to meet the one human being she felt sure would understand about Ormingat. This was Stella Dalrymple, who had featured in the newspapers her mother had given her to read. Stella had spoken of "starlight" when questioned about the Derwents' disappearance, and in such a tone that the reporter had woven a tale of extraterrestrial visitors that was just too near the truth. Stella obviously knew something. She might be Nesta's one chance of a friend in need. She could hold the key to this terrible riddle.

CHAPTER 19

Watchers in the Night

In London that Saturday evening, Jacob went to bed early. He was determined to be wide awake in the hours after midnight. He wanted to see whatever there was to see when the spaceship in York took flight and left Earth. His heart ached with the thought of it. Though it was not just one thought. There was pity and anxiety for Nesta, yes. The blue-gray eyes still haunted him. Then, the thought of all three Gwynns hurtling off into space was an uneasy one. And under all that there was envy. These were purebred Ormingatrig going to a place where they belonged. *Do I belong anywhere?* he wondered. *Who is Jacob Bradwell?*

After midnight, when Jacob got to the computer room, Steven was already there, looking somewhat dazed in front of the Brick's screen. He did not even speak as Jacob came and sat beside him.

"What's wrong, Dad? What is it?"

"Just look," said Steven. "Can't you see?"

Jacob leant forward to look more closely at the screen. The picture, bathed in reddish light, was of the Gwynns' back garden. To the left he could see, at an angle, the rear windows of the house and the projecting sides of the porch. Then there were the flower borders with shrubs at intervals around them. In the center was a stretch of lawn. And to the right, massive and ugly, was the gray stone frog.

"It's the Gwynns' back garden," said Jacob. "That is what we are supposed to be watching, isn't it?"

"And why are we watching it?" asked Steven through clenched teeth. "Think about it. Give it thought."

Jacob looked at the picture again, but still could reach no conclusion. "We are watching for the spaceship to leave Earth," he said, though this was so patently obvious he didn't see why it needed to be said.

"Yes," said Steven, "and leave Earth it will, less than two hours from now. I have made very sure of that. But it will leave without its passengers."

"How do you . . . ?" Jacob began, and then knew the answer to the question without asking it. "The frog's still in place! It's not lying on the grass! They'd need to move it to get in. And once they were in, there would be no one there to put it back."

"Exactly!" said Steven.

"But you said they would want to go," said Jacob. "You were sure they would."

"Want or not want," said his father, "they clearly are not going. My guess is that they have stayed behind because of their runaway daughter."

"Runaway daughter?" said Jacob, amazed. "You never told me Nesta had run away."

"It didn't seem necessary for you to know," said Steven. "I learnt of her disappearance on Thursday. There was no way I could help. But I naturally assumed that if she didn't turn up in time, they would go without her."

"Of course they couldn't, Dad," said Jacob. "You're not thinking straight. Would any right and responsible parents desert their child like that? Would you?"

"What a question!" said Steven indignantly. "Do you think I'm heartless?"

"If you're not," said Jacob, "why do you expect them to be?"

Steven sat back in his chair with a sigh. It was a mess, the biggest mess he had yet encountered. The parents were presumably looking for the daughter. The daughter was hiding goodness knows where. And the spaceship hidden under the frog was on a fast countdown to takeoff.

Then came another appalling thought. The frog was in the ship's flight path. What if it couldn't penetrate the stone? The beam had not penetrated it. What would happen to all that energy if it were hemmed back into the ground?

"What do we do now, Dad?" said Jacob anxiously.

"Nothing we can do—but watch," said his father. He kept to himself his own fears about what calamity might ensue when the countdown ended.

"They might do a last-minute run for it," said Jacob, staring toward the porch.

"They might," said Steven, "but I doubt it. I don't even know if it is possible. Doors are shut tight; shields are set up. Taking off is not accomplished in a matter of minutes."

The next two hours felt like forever. Steven and Jacob grew weary with watching. Steven was sick to his stomach, thinking silently of what might yet ensue.

And then came two o'clock.

Countdown complete.

At countdown plus one minute, there was suddenly a great heave from the frog, as if it had decided on a froglike leap commensurate with its size. It appeared to fling itself right up into the air and then it disappeared over the roof of the house. In the sky above it a red pinpoint of light left a trail across the clouds before it vanished.

"Gone," said Steven tersely.

"The frog?"

"The ship."

"But what has happened to the frog?" said Jacob. "Where is it now?"

Steven manipulated the Brick's controls till he was able to see the front of the Gwynns' house. There they saw the chaos the flying frog had caused. The road was gashed with great holes. A spurt of water from a main was shooting up into the lamplight. A policeman got out of a car and went toward the house.

Steven groaned. "More work for me," he said. "Always more work for me!"

The screen went blank, of its own accord and with no intervention from Steven.

Then on it appeared the message:

GO TO YOUR SHIP. YOUR ATTENDANCE IS REQUIRED.

Steven sighed. This was a not unexpected consequence of the events of the night. The ship without passengers could cause no end of trouble.

Jacob looked at his father anxiously. They had never been to the spaceship at dead of night. It was, to be honest, a bit scary. Yet he wouldn't think of holding back. He felt too deeply involved.

The first message disappeared off the top of the screen. A second one scrolled into place:

DO NOT BRING THE BOY. COME ALONE.

Jacob gave the screen a look of disgust. Why was he to be excluded? Did they think he was still a child? "The Cube said I should always come with you," he said. "So why not this time?"

Steven looked at him apologetically. "We can't go against orders," he said. "You must stay here."

"Till when?" said Jacob aggressively. "Doing what?"

Steven thought rapidly. "Stay by the Brick. I'll set it ready for you to watch. You will see me go into the spaceship and come out again. Then you can watch me safely home."

"What will you be doing inside the ship?" asked Jacob. "Why

is the Cube in such a hurry to see you at this time of night? Could it not have waited till tomorrow evening? And why does it not want me?"

Steven was too preoccupied to notice that his son was speaking as if the Cube were itself a person and not simply a channel of communication.

"I don't know," he said. "I simply don't know."

CHAPTER 20

Orders

The ship that left York is unmanned.

Steven looked up at the Cube, which at that moment was deep purple, not its usual reassuring green. That the Gwynn ship was empty was no surprise to him, but the circumstances of its departure were still uppermost in his mind.

His opening words were the speech for the defense.

"Before we begin," he said, "let me make it clear that I know that things have gone wrong. But I am in no way responsible. When the frog flew over the rooftop, I was as much taken by surprise as anyone could be."

The Cube had faded to a less livid shade as soon as Steven began to speak, but at these words it went completely dead, as if it had blown a fuse.

Steven pulled on the lever he knew should summon the communicator back to life.

Nothing happened.

He leant forward and vigorously wrenched the lever from side to side.

The Cube glowed mauve but said nothing.

"Why am I here? Why have you summoned me?" said Steven, remembering that it was best to ask basic questions if the communication seemed slow.

The color of the Cube returned to its normal hue, so clearly that was the right thing to do.

Steven was still intensely worried about the frog. So he added nothing to his original question and just waited to see what the machine would say. An extended silence eventually forced him to prod the communicator's memory.

Keep it simple, Sterekanda. Say something that will provoke an answer.

"What about the frog?" he said. "Is it a cause for concern?"

We know nothing of any frog. Data on the subject of flying frogs is not available. Relevance is not understood. The ship that left York is unmanned.

Steven then realized how little aware the communicator was of all the commotion at Linden Drive. Quick thinking made him decide not to pursue this: more knowledge might well mean more work!

"The ship is on course," said Steven. "I checked its flight path. In spite of everything, it is on course."

The ship is unmanned.

"The Gwynns must still be searching for their daughter," said Steven. "They must have found it impossible to leave without her."

And now they will find it impossible to leave at all. Such are the rules. Earth has claimed them. Earth must keep them.

"So there is nothing left to do," said Steven, content to let it go at that.

You must watch the house in York and report how things are. We do not wish to have unforeseen dangers.

"For how long?" said Steven, immediately worried that the communicator was going to demand too much of him. But at least if he were to be the sole observer, he would have some control over what went into the report. (No frogs!)

Till you know all we need to know.

"What do we need to know?"

Anything that further threatens our security. When the girl is found, you must discover where she has been. You must find out if any outsider has been given secret information.

That sounded a very tall order, but worse was to come.

You must test the attitudes and emotions of her parents and bring influence to bear on them so that whatever of Ormingat remains will be lost.

"How do I do all that?" said Steven harshly.

Begin by eavesdropping.

Steven decided to pursue this no further.

"I should perhaps go now," he said. "Valuable watching time is being wasted. My son is waiting for me."

Not yet. There is one other thing here that you must do. It is of supreme importance and will need your undivided attention. That is why you had to come alone.

"Yes?" said Steven, his mouth dry already and his nerves stretched.

You must adjust the clock in this ship. Set its return for the first of March. That will give you time to finish your work with the Gwynns, and to deal with the problem of Stella Dalrymple.

This left Steven gasping. Reset the clock? Deal with Stella Dalrymple?

"I need time to think."

Resetting the clock comes first.

"I really do need time to think," said Steven anxiously. "Let me go home and return tomorrow. I have data there that will assist me—I can check on the method I used to reset the clock in York."

Resetting must be done now.

It was as if the Cube could recognize his special pleading.

"I haven't got time to do it now," said Steven firmly. "I expected this to be a short visit. You gave me no proper warning."

Resetting must be done now.

"I can't and won't do it," said Steven. "You must give me at least until tomorrow night."

You can and will reset the clock before you leave the ship.

Steven turned toward the wall where the door should be, but

no door was in evidence. The door device was totally under the command of the Cube.

"Don't be so tiresome," he said angrily.

Do your work, Sterekanda. The quicker you start, the sooner you'll finish.

The voice of the Cube had become parental: kindly in tone, but rigidly determined. Steven knew then that there was no point in further argument. If he wanted to leave the ship, he would have to do as he was bid.

Adjusting the clock was easier this time. He remembered clearly how he had carried out the operation on the clock in York. And here there was the advantage of having the instrument directly under his hands.

After thirty minutes he was able to turn to the Cube and say, "The adjustment is complete."

From the Cube, a ray beamed momentarily down on the face of the clock as if checking the accuracy of Steven's statement. Ormingat, after two hundred and fifty uneventful years of space travel, was learning not to trust.

"So what about Stella Dalrymple?" said Steven.

You must pay her a visit. Deal with her direct. Make sure that she ceases to believe the things the boy Tonitheen told her. Work on her mind.

"And what about Javayl?" said Steven. He merely meant, what should I tell my son about all of this? The communicator understood the question differently.

Javayl comes with you, of course. You come home together.

CHAPTER 21

Eavesdropping

Left alone in the workroom, Jacob moved into his father's chair in front of the Brick. He was no expert in the use of it, but he knew enough of the fundamentals to be able to seek, find, and follow. Steven changed the setting before leaving so that the screen showed an overview of Swains Lane. It was child's play to zoom in and out, to drag the image to one side or the other. But Jacob was not content with any of that.

You can watch for me. You can look after the Brick.

Big deal!

It was too simple a bribe.

Jacob carefully considered the controls and decided to experiment. He found the whole of the British Isles, with all its colored counties. Next he zoomed in on the city of York and its suburbs, then on to the estate to the north where the Gwynns lived, and finally right into the back garden from which the frog had so recently leapt.

All the activity that had been in evidence before Steven changed the setting was still there. An ambulance and two fire engines had arrived, but it became evident that they were not needed. The water hydrant was turned off. Soon the only real activity was in the back garden. A small group was gathered round the spot where the pond had been. Jacob concluded that they must be investigators of some sort. Three other people, two men and a woman, stopped briefly in the garden before entering the house by the back door.

Jacob deduced that these must be Mr. and Mrs. Gwynn and someone interested either in the explosive frog or in the whereabouts of their daughter. Perhaps both.

He manipulated the controls hopefully and at last managed to get into the living room, where the Gwynns were talking to the man. It was frustrating that the Brick could not transmit any sound back to him. It was all very well being a fly on the wall, but not knowing what was being said definitely hindered the usefulness of the position.

The older man went out of the room and a young policeman in uniform came in and sat down. The Gwynns soon left him sitting by himself, obviously on duty.

The Brick could take Jacob no further and tell him no more. He looked at the policeman dozing uncomfortably on the upright chair he had either chosen or been invited to occupy. He yawned and almost fell asleep himself.

Then, just after three o'clock, the screen flashed with sudden activity. The living room door opened, the young policeman stood to attention, and in came the Gwynns. Jacob was instantly alert and attentive to the on-screen movements.

He bent over the controls again and zoomed in on Alison Gwynn's face. She looked happy. That could mean only one thing: Nesta was safe and had got in touch.

"And what do you think *you're* doing?"

Jacob jumped at the sound of his father's voice. Steven had come very quietly into the room, not wanting his footsteps to waken anyone else in the house. He came closer to the Brick and saw the picture on-screen.

"Why have you changed the view? Can you not carry out a

simple instruction? Don't you know what damage you can do? Get off my seat. Get out of my way."

Steven had practically run all the way from Swains Lane. He was out of breath and in a high state of irritation. "Eavesdropping!" he said crossly. "Idle curiosity."

Then he stopped himself saying more as he realized that eavesdropping was now to be the order of the day. A difficult order to put into action, given the Brick's lack of sound. He pulled a lever and said crossly, "I can't listen to what I can't hear."

Jacob watched the screen, where the picture suddenly had one word starkly imposed over it:

IMPROVISE.

"How do I do that, mute object?" said Steven irritably.

USE SPEAKERS FROM ANOTHER SYSTEM.

Steven looked at his Earth computer on the other side of the room. It was equipped with two speakers plugged into the port that led to the modem.

"It can't be done," he said. "The systems are totally incompatible."

LIP-READ.

"I wouldn't know how."

Jacob looked from his father to the screen and then back. "Just watch, Dad," he said. "Stop arguing and watch. I have made sense of what I've seen. You might not be able to lip-read, but you can tell from people's faces what they're thinking—and you can watch where they go and what they do."

The communicator seemed to have digested this advice. It seized on the most useful of Jacob's words:

WATCH.

The letters appeared on the screen for just a few seconds and then disappeared to return Steven to the view of the Gwynns' living room. Once again the Gwynns left the policeman sitting alone.

"I'll split the screen," said Steven, half to himself and half to his son, who had been tacitly restored to favor.

"To follow the Gwynns?" said Jacob.

"Not necessary," said Steven, "and not helpful because we are stuck with not being able to hear what they say. No. I want to keep my eye on what is happening outside."

Jacob looked down at his watch and said, stifling a yawn, "It's twenty past four, Dad. There'll be nothing to see for a few more hours."

Steven nevertheless took a look at the back garden. A strong spotlight was trained on the pond. Two workers were busy there, sifting soil and passing small objects to a man sitting cross-legged on a groundsheet. A zoom in on their faces showed that they were all bored and that the objects were probably mind-numbingly insignificant.

For the next three hours, nothing happened at all. Jacob sat in the armchair and fell asleep. Steven stayed at his post and dozed, coming fully awake every time he began to slip sideways.

At seven-thirty Jacob woke up, hurried over to the camp stool, and said, "Has anything happened? Have I missed anything? Where are the Gwynns?"

"They're probably fast asleep in bed."

"How do you know?" said Jacob.

"They haven't left the house," said Steven. "No one has entered the house. Yet they were happy enough. My guess is that Nesta is on her way home and they know exactly when she is due to arrive. The worry has been lifted. They're bound to be exhausted. So they'll have gone to sleep."

When daylight came, there was activity once more. The Gwynns came into the living room, looking drained and certainly not as well rested as Steven had thought they would be. When they went to the kitchen, the young constable followed them, and all three took a silent look out at the back garden, where the workers were still excavating as carefully as archaeologists on some ancient dig.

By nine-thirty the Gwynns were clearly ready for the day, but neither they nor the constable left the house.

"Jacob?" Lydia called up the stairs. "Are you not ready for church yet? We don't want to be late."

She had not called her son down to breakfast because she had some idea that he had been up late the night before, messing about with that computer.

"Do I have to go?" said Jacob to his father.

"I think so," said Steven. "We can talk about it in depth another time, but for now just go."

Jacob's thoughts had been far less philosophical than his father's answer gave him credit for. He had simply wanted to play hooky so as not to miss the excitement.

So Steven was alone when the older man of the night before returned to the Gwynns'. There was a short conversation between the three of them, but Steven had no idea what it might be about.

By the time Jacob returned, another policeman had taken over from the constable who had worked the night shift, and the older man had gone.

"I was wishing I could lip-read," said Steven. "There was no guessing what they were saying."

"The older man must be a senior policeman, plain clothes," said Jacob, "and they were obviously discussing something about Nesta's return."

"Yes," drawled Steven sarcastically.

"Well, it's obvious, isn't it? What else would they want to talk about?"

CHAPTER 22

York Station

Just after half-past twelve, there was more activity. The older man, who by now had been accorded the rank of inspector by Steven and Jacob, returned in a police car. Then he accompanied the Gwynns to their own car and got in the backseat.

"Where can they be going?" said Jacob.

"To the police station? To help the police with their inquiries?"

"But then they would be in the police car, not their own," Jacob objected.

The inspector's car also set off, just after the Gwynns'.

Steven bent over the Brick and manipulated the buttons till he had the trace viewer set up. It would not be as difficult as directing a spaceship all the way from Edinburgh to Casselton, but it required dexterity to be able to follow the cars and keep them center screen. They headed down into York, past the Museum Gardens, and over the Lendal Bridge.

"Not the police station," said Steven. "The railway station. Now this will take a bit of doing. When they've parked the car, we'll have to follow them inside. That's clearly where they must be going."

"Why?" said Jacob. "Why would they want to go there?"

"Either to catch a train," said Steven, "or to meet a train."

"They're meeting a train with Nesta on it," said Jacob, suddenly inspired. "So let's not follow them to the car park. Let's get a probe directly into the station and see what trains are due to arrive."

"Okay, okay," said his father. "Good thinking."

The screen now showed the station's main hall: shops, restaurants, waiting rooms, all presided over by the electronic arrivals and departures board.

"Which train?" said Jacob. Several were listed on the board, some with platform numbers, some without. The board was constantly changing.

Without a word, Steven split the screen so that the top left-hand corner had a square with a fixed focus on the indicator board.

"You keep watching that," he said to his son, "and I'll concentrate on the entrance. That way I can pick them up and follow them onto the platform, and you can check where the train is coming from."

He had just finished speaking when the Gwynns arrived, followed closely by the inspector, who spoke to them and then was clearly dismissed as Matthew and Alison strode well in front of him onto the platform.

"Platform three," said Steven.

"That's the London train," said Jacob, looking at the notice board. "Coming from Edinburgh. It's running late."

He was getting tired of watching the board so conscientiously. "We can switch that off now, can't we?" he said. "Then we can both watch the Gwynns more easily."

"Not yet," said his father. "Keep watching till the train arrives."

"There'll be nothing more to see," said Jacob.

"Never mind," said Steven impatiently. "Keep watching anyway."

He would really have preferred to be alone in the room at this moment. What he was doing demanded total concentration.

After a short while, for some reason Steven could not fathom, the Gwynns left the platform where they had been standing and hurried across the bridge, the inspector following them. To keep them within range of the trace required all the deftness of touch that Steven had developed with years of experience.

"Go on, then," he said as he managed to get a view of the other side of the bridge. "Tell me why they did that."

"Announcement explaining that the train they are waiting for will be arriving at a different platform," said Jacob.

"You know that?"

"I know that," said Jacob. "Quite simple, really. It just came up on the notice board."

The train came in and drew to a halt. Steven pressed the button to cancel the split screen. Now father and son were both eagerly watching the passengers alighting. There were not very many.

One was a girl in a red coat. She waved like mad at Matthew and Alison and ran toward them.

"That's it," said Jacob, relieved to see the family reunited. He was pleased to see Nesta safe and well. But now the inspector seemed to be talking to them all rather insistently.

"They need protection," said Jacob.

"Not possible," his father replied. "We don't know what is being said and we don't know exactly what we would be protecting them from."

"They could be in trouble," said Jacob anxiously. "I don't like the look of that inspector, or whatever he is."

"Athelerane will have to manage that herself. She can. She is the stronger of that duo."

"That's not fair on Matthew," said Jacob, ignoring the name his father had just given to Matthew's wife, but knowing exactly whom he meant.

"Not really," said Steven. "Matthew has greater wisdom. Alison has the talent for mind-fencing. In this situation it will work better than the Brick would. We can only hope she hasn't lost it yet."

"Lost it?" said Jacob.

"Oh, yes," said Steven. "Now that she is no longer Ormingatrig, the talent will go."

He turned his attention to the train once more, passengers getting on, doors closing. The trace scoured the length of the platform.

"Ah!" he said. "There's something *you've* missed."

"What?"

"All of the travelers who got off the train are heading for the exit—except one."

"What is he doing?" asked Jacob.

"*She*. Exactly what we are doing," said Steven. "She is watching the Gwynns, or maybe their daughter."

Steven zoomed in on a woman still standing on the platform, some distance from the Gwynns but clearly looking at them. She was dressed in a brown tweed coat and had a scarf flung over her shoulders. As her face came into sharper focus, Steven saw the coppery hair, the amber eyes, and the concerned expression of someone he instantly recognized.

This was a face he had been shown in the ship, the face of someone he had been told to "deal with." It was with no sense of triumph that he pronounced her name. There was alarm in his voice.

"Stella Dalrymple! What does she know of the Gwynns? Why is she here in York?"

"What do we do now?" said Jacob. He had heard of Stella. He knew she was connected with the Derwents in Belthorp. This was the woman who had caused all the trouble by using the wrong words at the wrong time—"Starlight, perhaps." If she also knew about Nesta, she was clearly one of the most dangerous contacts on the planet.

"We could ignore it," said his father, knowing that Jacob would want it to go in the report and only too well aware of what over-reporting had done the last time.

He took his view back to the Gwynns and was satisfied to see the inspector turn his back on them and walk quickly away. Athelerane had clearly been able to do what was required.

"I might not have been clever enough to observe the other passenger," said Steven thoughtfully. "The whole thing could be more bother than it's worth."

"We don't know that," said Jacob. "You were told to report. So you must report. What I meant was—do we carry on watching the Gwynns? Or do we watch Mrs. Dalrymple? And what use will it all be anyway?"

"Small cogs in a big machine," said Steven. "That's what we are. The one thing we do not need to know is the answer to the question 'What use?' But you're right to wonder what we should do next."

"Ask the Brick," said Jacob, nodding toward the lever that would permit them to speak to the instrument.

"No need, *Javayl ban*," said Steven with a sigh. "I know the answer. We must go to our own spaceship and talk to the communicator. The Brick, after all, has bricklike qualities that render it of limited use."

"It's Sunday," said Jacob anxiously. "Dinner will be ready soon."

"Then our visit to the ship will have to wait," said Steven, and immediately thought that the delay was not such a bad idea.

As if on cue, a voice from downstairs called, "Are you two going to stay up there all day? Dinner's on the table. Come down now!"

It was unusual for Lydia to sound impatient, but mealtimes were important to her. All of the Bradwells, from the oldest to the youngest, knew that. So Steven and Jacob hurried down to dinner.

Steven stopped briefly to turn off the screen, catching just one last glimpse of the Gwynn family as they left the station.

"We will see them again," said Jacob.

"But not too soon," said Steven tersely. "I want to think this one out."

"So when do we tell about Stella Dalrymple?" said Jacob with complete disregard for the mood his father was in.

"In a day or two," said Steven smoothly. "Let the dust settle. There's no point in rushing things."

But never far from his mind were the last words the Cube had spoken before he left the spaceship:

Javayl comes with you, of course. You come home together.

That was the real problem. Set next to that, Stella Dalrymple's involvement was trivial.

CHAPTER 23

The Homecoming

Alison knew that her Ormingat powers were fading, but with determination she summoned up all her strength to get rid of the nosy inspector. She simply told him to go and leave them, but on the level of mind-fencing she made him believe that nothing really important had occurred. He had been on the point of questioning Nesta and was even talking about calling in the social services when Alison had fixed her gaze on him, told him very firmly that he was no longer needed, and quietly ordered him to be on his way.

She had no idea that her efforts had been anxiously watched over by Steven and Jacob, scanning a screen in the upper room of a house two hundred miles away.

Nesta walked from the station between her parents, holding on to both of them and determined never to leave them again. She had achieved her aim. They would never, ever leave this Earth. Ormingat could be forgotten.

"It's been hard, you know," said Alison as they drove back home. "You can't imagine how painful it's been."

She was sitting in the backseat, still holding Nesta's hand. Matthew was content to be chauffeur so that mother and daughter could sit together. There was still a lot of healing to do.

"I know, Mom," said Nesta. "I didn't want to hurt you, but it was all too much. How could you expect me to leave this world in that tiny spaceship and stop being human? That's what it would have meant, you know, however you try to make it seem normal. It wasn't normal at all."

"For us it was," said Matthew. "That's where we went wrong. We thought just being our child would be enough to make it— well, reasonably easy."

"Easy!" said Nesta, indignation overcoming affection. "It was impossible. You should have known it would be."

"There, there," said her mother anxiously. "It's over now, and probably best forgotten, but first we must know where you've been and what you've said to people. We can't start over again without wiping the slate clean."

All her parents knew was that she had spent one night with Stella Dalrymple, the kind stranger who had phoned them and told them that their daughter was safe; the very kind stranger who had escorted their child to the railway station at York, saying farewell to her on the train so that no one outside her family need ever know where she had been.

"Can it wait till later?" said Nesta. "I'm still so tired."

"You're tired!" said Matthew over his shoulder, with a vehemence that was unusual in him. "You're tired! How do you think we feel? Never for an instant have you tried to see our point of view. We've been through hell searching for you. And never in a lifetime will you know what we have lost."

Alison gave him a look of alarm.

Nesta began to weep quietly.

"Leave it," said Alison. "Leave it for now. We are all overwrought."

Matthew said no more, but it pierced him to think of the slate being wiped so clean. He was not even sure that he could manage it. And what would happen now? Even if they could persuade themselves to forget about Ormingat, would that be the end of it?

Nothing more was said in the car.

Even when they arrived home and settled into the comfort of their living room, the subject was left severely alone. Alison made tea and sandwiches.

"No Sunday dinner today," she said with a wan smile. "I didn't get round to making it."

It was Matthew who brought up the topic first. He regretted his outburst. He loved his daughter too much to want to make her unhappy. As they sat eating the meal and drinking their tea, he looked across at her and said gently, "It would help us to know where you have been since Wednesday. Four nights away from home is something any twelve-year-old would be expected to account for, Nesta. We know why you went, but we really do need to know *where* you went."

He was the right one to put the question. Alison would have phrased it wrongly and Nesta would have put up a barrier.

"I don't want anyone to get into trouble because of me," she said.

"No one will," said Matthew.

"What about the police?"

"They will never be told anything," said Matthew. "There's no fear of that. We asked them to find you. It was a mistake, but not too serious a one. Your mother saw to that."

Nesta smiled obliquely at her mother before giving her full attention to her father again.

"And you wouldn't get on to the school either, would you? Or anybody's parents?"

"No," said Matthew slowly, but he did wonder what was coming next.

"Promise," said Nesta.

"I promise," said her father. "Neither your mother nor I will ever tell anyone whatever you tell us now."

"I stayed with Amy," said Nesta. "I stayed three nights in her garage. She looked after me."

"I knew!" said her mother. "I just knew you would be with Amy Brown. If only we'd known her address!"

Nesta shivered. *Thank goodness you didn't! You might have got me back in time and forced me into the spaceship, though I'd have put up a struggle, no mistake!*

"What did you tell Amy?" said Matthew anxiously.

"That you were going home to Boston and that I didn't want to go there."

"And that's all?"

"What else could I tell her?" said Nesta huffily. "Even if I weren't keeping your secrets, do you think she'd have believed in fiddly little spaceships and people diminishing? She'd have thought I wasn't all there."

"So how did you end up in Belthorp with Mrs. Dalrymple?" said her father, no longer interested in Amy's part in what he supposed both girls would regard as some sort of adventure. He deduced that camping out in the garage might even have been a game they enjoyed. It sounded like fun!

"I couldn't stay at Amy's on Saturday because her brother comes home at weekends and keeps his bike in the garage."

"But to go all the way to Belthorp to find Mrs. Dalrymple?" said Matthew. "That was a bit much, wasn't it? How did you even think of it?"

"Please, Dad, try to understand me. I had to go somewhere, and I thought I might be found if I wandered about here in York. Then I was drawn toward Stella Dalrymple. I wanted to meet the only person on Earth who knew that Thomas and his father were aliens; I felt as if she might somehow be able to give me some sort of clue."

"And did she?" said Matthew.

Alison looked keenly at her daughter, eager to know how she would answer this.

"She loved the Derwents," said Nesta. "She didn't care about anything as long as they were safe and happy. She wasn't even all that interested in Ormingat. She somehow made it feel not so fantastic. But she did tell me not to talk about it to anyone, and not even to let anyone know that we had ever met. Keeping it a secret was what was really important to her."

"And that helped?" said her mother.

"Yes," said Nesta. "I think it did. It means just what you said. We can wipe the slate clean. We can forget all about it."

"There must be no more running away," said Alison, speaking like any Earth mother to her wayward child. "Not ever again."

Nesta's eyes darkened to a deep shade of gray. She tugged a strand of hair across her lip. The look she gave her mother was not pleasant or submissive. She was nearly thirteen and mature for her age. The past few days had made sure of that.

"I didn't enjoy it," she snapped. "I didn't run away for fun."

"Don't push it," said her father, feeling irritation rising again. "Just don't push it. When you think how much you have suffered, have the grace to realize that we are suffering too."

Nesta smiled as sweetly as she could and took her father's hand in hers. "I am sorry, you know," she said in a conciliatory voice. "Wiping the slate clean doesn't mean I'm not sorry."

Matthew sighed and said no more.

CHAPTER 24

See to It!

It was Tuesday evening before Steven and Jacob went once more up Swains Lane to report to the spaceship. The Cube heard them out and was silent for at least half an hour. During that time, Jacob was tempted to speak but Steven's look warned him to be silent. The communicator must be left to assimilate the knowledge laid before it.

Suddenly there was a whir and silver zigzags crossed inside the Cube before its speech emerged.

Too many things have gone wrong. You have failed to stem the flow. You must see to it. You must put right the errors.

Steven and Jacob looked at one another, wondering what putting right the errors would involve. Jacob was rapidly coming round to his father's point of view that the communicator often expected too much of them. Steven had dutifully given the information about Stella's appearance on the platform at York Station.

"There was nothing I could do to prevent things going wrong. I carried out my instructions; I passed on my observations. And you have to know that I did a brilliant job in ensuring that Vateelin and Tonitheen made it to their spaceship in time," Steven protested. It was important to remind the Cube of this success; it might mitigate the York failure.

One simple thing might have been sufficient. You should have protected the coat on the hospital bed. You should have rendered it unnoticeable. It was well within your power.

"Speed was important," said Steven. "A few seconds more and our friends would not have made it to their ship in time."

Yet it was a thought, a tormenting thought. If only he had taken the time and effort to protect that coat! It was the one area in which he and the Brick were absolute experts. Some nurse would have removed it from the bed quite absently, to tidy up. Another might have put it in the lost property, to be auctioned off for some charity at a later date.

"It would still have been necessary to account for a missing child," said Steven defensively. "The coat was not the be-all and end-all."

Cry not over the milk that has spilt.

Steven grimaced at the machine's crude translation of a proverb it could barely understand. Did they have milk on Ormingat?

"So?" he said.

Go and see Stella Dalrymple. Ensure that she poses no future threat.

"And the Gwynns? What about them?"

For this the rule must be changed.

"Which rule?"

You must make personal contact so that your influence will be felt. Go and see them. Let them know how complete the break is. Make them understand the importance of forgetting. Make them forget. But first, find out about their knowledge of Stella Dalrymple.

Jacob had sat by his father's side listening to every word. "Can you really make them forget that they are from Ormingat? You could not make me forget anything as important as that!"

Steven pulled the lever to exclude the Cube from their conversation. "I do have powers," he said. "Powers I have never used. I will be truthful with you—I don't know how well they work. My expertise is with the Brick. The rest is questionable. To my mind it will all depend upon how much resistance I meet with."

He pulled the lever back to reestablish communication with the Cube.

You have made Javayl to understand.

"That was my purpose," said Steven, without actually confirming or denying how much or how little Jacob now knew and understood.

So go and do what must be done.

Steven grimaced at Jacob, who merely shrugged in return.

Remember well that all must be complete before the month of February is fled.

"Very poetic," snapped Steven, irritated at the mention, however indirectly, of the date of their departure. Jacob knew nothing of it yet, and his father did not know how, or when, or whether to tell him.

Back in the workroom, after a late tea, Steven and Jacob were once more seated in front of the Brick. On screen was the village of Belthorp. Steven focused upon the door of Stella Dalrymple's cottage.

"Do we go in? Can we see her?" said Jacob eagerly.

"Just briefly," said Steven. "I want to see her home before we visit. I want to see her moving about in it, living her life."

The beam was trained on the windowpane and then the Bradwells had a view of Stella's sitting room. No one there—a log fire burning, two shaded lamps giving the place a burnished glow. In front of the settee there was a table with a tray on it, a patterned china cup and saucer, an empty plate beside it. Then the lady of the house came in, unmistakably Stella, the light glinting in her coppery hair. She picked up the tray and went out again.

On the mantelpiece were photos: one of a young man in academic robes, a degree portrait. Another had the same young man standing by a younger Stella in her wedding dress. The other pictures were of Thomas Derwent at different ages—one with Patrick beside him, another with Stella, and two more of Thomas on his own.

"We know her now," said Steven, withdrawing the probe.

"We know her?"

"We know all we need to know. At half term you and I will pay her that visit and tidy up loose ends. Till then, we can leave her to get peacefully on with her life."

"So we wait till half term before going north?" said Jacob.

"It's practical, if you are to go with me. Your mother doesn't like you missing school."

"And will that give you enough time to finish everything? The Cube said you must be all done before the end of February."

"Before the first of March," said Steven, correcting him.

"And in the meantime, do we watch the Gwynns?" said Jacob. He was eager to see Nesta again. The eagerness showed just a little too much.

Steven smiled. "We'll look in from time to time," he said. "It's only another three weeks. Then we'll be on their doorstep, presenting ourselves in whatever guise seems best by then."

Steven set the screen to roll back into the Brick. "Go downstairs now, Javayl. I'll soon follow. Let's have an evening away from this."

Jacob turned to go, but suddenly he stopped in the doorway. A strange thought had come to him. "Why before the first of March?" he said. "What is so special about that date?"

"I'll tell you later," said Steven. "It's too late now."

The one question that Steven did not want to answer should never have been asked. He was becoming increasingly aware that his influence over his son's thoughts was weakening. The shield was still there, but the mind-fencing was encountering opposition.

CHAPTER 25

Stella's Unwelcome Visitor

At teatime on Wednesday the newspaper shop in Belthorp was busy.

"That'll be eleven pounds eighty altogether, Mrs. Budd," said Sam Swanson after pondering over the entries in the book.

"All that money on newspapers," said Mary Budd, taking two ten-pound notes from her purse. "It's not all that long since you could keep a family for a week on that!"

"Time goes by," said the newsagent, handing his customer her change. "Seems no time since I was a lad delivering the papers and here I am with two kids of me own nearly ready to take over!"

Philip and Anthony had just come home from school and were behind the corner counter looking for the Wednesday comics before going upstairs for their tea. Mickey Trent was with them, his back to the shop.

At the main counter, three women with children were waiting to be served. As Mary was about to leave the shop, yet another customer entered. This was not a villager. Mary stepped to one side, deciding to stop and see who it might be. All of the women looked askance at him. Sam smiled at them, as much as to say, I'll get rid of this one and then we can get on with our business. The youngsters always dillydallied, so there was no harm in allowing the stranger to jump the queue.

"Can I help you?" said Sam.

Rupert Shawcross smiled politely. If he'd been wearing a hat, he would probably have doffed it. It was part of his technique to be smooth. This was not his first visit to the village: he had been there once before, to interview Stella Dalrymple. He was not a journalist nosing out a story. He was a government investigator. His office in Manchester specialized in collecting information about possible extraterrestrial visitors; hence his interest in Mrs. Dalrymple, the lady whose neighbors had so mysteriously disappeared.

"I'll take a packet of those cigars," he said, indicating a pack on the shelf behind the newsagent. "And a box of chocolates. They're for Mrs. Dalrymple. Do you happen to know what sort she likes?"

The women inspected him more closely.

"I'm a friend of hers," said Rupert, stretching the truth. He had only met her once, and then she had given him short shrift!

"You'll not have seen her for some time, then?" said Sam, just a shade suspicious of the stranger. "We don't get many strangers in the village."

This was Rupert's opportunity to inquire about any other strangers, but he missed it. One of the mothers joined in the conversation, saying, "I *knew* I'd seen you somewhere recently. You were at Stella's just a couple of weeks ago."

At the corner counter, Mickey Trent kept his head well down. He had met Mr. Shawcross and he didn't want to meet him again. He had come snooping, asking questions about Mickey's best friend, Thomas Derwent.

"Yes," said Rupert, making the best of this. "I was up here making inquiries about the Derwents. That is how Mrs. Dalrymple and I became acquainted. I just thought I'd pop back to see how she was getting on. I don't suppose she's had any more visitors?"

"Strangers, you mean," said Sam, "like yourself?"

"There was that girl," said Mary Budd helpfully, "the one I saw at the station. Mrs. Dalrymple was taking her home to Casselton."

Anthony had lost interest in the conversation of the other two boys and was making his way behind the main counter toward the door to their flat. He stopped as he heard talk about "that girl" and "Mrs. Dalrymple."

"We saw her," he said excitedly, "Phil and me. Mickey took her across from the bus stop to Mrs. Dalrymple's house. Didn't you, Mickey?"

Mickey turned round reluctantly.

"Didn't I what?" he said.

"Take that girl to Mrs. Dalrymple's the other night. Phil and I saw you."

"Mickey!" said Rupert Shawcross delightedly. "Perhaps we should have a little talk."

"Sorry, no!" said Mickey. "I'm in a hurry, and in any case I don't want to talk to you, and don't come to our house because I'll tell my mam not to let you in."

He flushed. It was the first time in his life he had ever been so pointedly rude to anybody. Without another word, he rushed out of the shop.

"Well!" said Mrs. Tolent, leaning heavily on the handles of the pushchair she was holding. "What can you make of that?" Her gaze was full on the stranger.

"Not a lot," he said rather feebly. "I did ask him a few questions about Thomas last time I was here. It's my job, you see. Thomas Derwent is a missing youngster. We are still pursuing inquiries."

"The lad'll be upset," said another woman. "They were very friendly, you know."

But Rupert Shawcross was already following another line of thought. Who was the girl?

"You can't go wrong with Black Magic," said Sam, placing a large box on the counter next to the cigars.

"That'll be fine," said Rupert absently. He paid for his purchases, slipped them into his briefcase, and was glad to get out of the shop.

"Yes?" said Stella, opening the door just a fraction. She had seen Rupert coming and was ready for him. She had as little wish to converse with him as Mickey had, but adults are constrained to be civil, most of the time.

"Can I come in for a minute?" said Rupert. "It won't take long."

Stella smiled slightly. "I have work to do," she said. "I can give you maybe ten minutes, and a cup of tea if you'd like one."

An outright refusal to speak to the investigator might not be the thing to do. Stella wanted to keep abreast of what he had managed to find out. So far as she was concerned, the situation had become very sensitive since Nesta's visit. It was important to know whether the moles of Manchester had succeeded in establishing a connection between Thomas and Nesta. It seemed unlikely, but Stella was very cautious.

"That's kind of you," said Rupert, taking the chocolates from his case. "Brought you a present."

"I hope that's not some sort of bribe," said Stella, raising an eyebrow. "Still, I can run to one or two biscuits."

Stella at that moment reminded Rupert of his cousin Audrey, who always made him feel as if she were mocking him in a kindly way. To Rupert, who was devoid of humor, it was puzzling. He sat down and listened to the clock ticking till Stella brought in the tray.

"Now," she said. "Does this mean you've had some word of Thomas?"

"No," said Rupert dolefully. "The trail has gone completely cold, I'm afraid. I was really just wanting to check if you had heard anything."

"Sorry," said Stella. "No word here."

"You had another young visitor the other day, so I'm told," said Rupert. He bit hard on a custard cream as he waited for her reply.

"Where on earth did you get that insignificant snippet of news from?" said Stella, immediately alert but genuinely puzzled.

"A lady in the newsagent's mentioned seeing you take a girl to the Casselton train. As soon as I heard your name, I wondered if this girl could in any way be connected with Thomas."

"What a daft conclusion to come to," said Stella. "Why should she be? I do have visitors, you know."

"Yes, I know," said Rupert. "I suppose it's grasping at straws. It intrigued me that Mickey Trent was upset when it was mentioned. That young man has taken a bit of a dislike to me, I'm sorry to say."

"Well," said Stella, "the daughter of a friend of mine paid me a visit. That's all. As for Mickey, he met her at the bus stop and walked her to my door. Maybe he felt a bit embarrassed about that. You know what boys are like."

That, if Rupert had any sensitivity, should have been the end of the matter. Stella certainly hoped and expected that it would be.

But he persisted.

"What is her name?" he said.

"Whose name?"

"The name of the girl who came to see you."

Stella put her cup down noisily on the saucer. "Mr. Shawcross!" she said. "I am not going to be interrogated about any visitor who happens to come to my house. It is none of your business what her name is."

Rupert crumbled a scone on his plate. "I have a job to do," he said anxiously. "You must let me be the judge of what is my business. If you have nothing to hide, this child's name is totally unimportant."

"Names are always important," said Stella. "We carry them from the cradle to the grave and beyond. There can be nothing more important than that."

Rupert shook his head.

"I think you'd better go now," said Stella. "I really have a lot of work to do, and there's nothing more I can say to you."

"The girl's name?" said Rupert with one last stupid effort. "I like to cover the ground thoroughly. This visit has really produced nothing else of note."

"The girl's name, and where she lives and why she was visiting me?" said Stella, sounding reasonable.

"That sort of thing," said Rupert obtusely.

"You must be joking! Have you never heard of civil liberties? Please leave. Leave now."

Rupert stood up and fastened his coat. He reached for his briefcase.

"And you'd better take your chocolates too," said Stella, thrusting the box toward him. "I could never bring myself to eat them, and I do hate waste."

CHAPTER 26

February Fair Maids

There were two cakes, one on either side of the table, each bearing ten candles surrounding a sugar snowdrop. This was the ritual for the start of February. In the church's calendar it might be Candlemas Day. For the poet, it was the month of snowdrops. For the Bradwells, February the second was the twins' birthday. And this year they were ten.

Lydia lit the candles one at a time, going back and forth from one cake to the other so that both were equal. She had to stop twice to strike another match. Then every candle was lit. The curtains were already closed because the day had been dark and dusk had come early. Lydia turned out the light so that the twenty little candles glowed more brightly. Then she said, "Now, my February fair maids, let's see which of you can blow out your candles first!"

Beth and Josie stood over their cakes and each gave one powerful puff. Then all of the candles were out and it would have taken a gimlet eye to decide who was the winner. In near darkness, the others at the table applauded. Steven reached over and switched on the light.

"I won!" said Josie.

"No, you didn't. I did."

"I did!"

"You didn't!"

"Cool it, my children. You both won," said their father. "It was definitely a dead heat!"

"Did you remember to make a wish?" said Kerry, careful to look very quickly from one to the other so that it would be clear that she was addressing both of them.

"I wished—" Josie began and then stopped as her mother put a finger to her lips and said, "Oh no! No, no! You must never tell your wish or it won't come true."

Next to Kerry, Jacob sat silent. *Wishes don't come true anyway,* he thought. *Things just happen or they don't.* If anyone had looked his way, they would have seen his cynical expression. But no one did: he might as well not have been there.

Uncle Mark had not been able to come: Aunt Jane was in hospital having her toenails cut. (That unkind remark was courtesy of Steven, who never believed in any of Aunt Jane's illnesses.) Mark had sent an expensive baby doll for each of his nieces. At first they had pretended to be disgusted at such a childish present, but secretly they were pleased. The dolls looked like real babies and were soft and cuddly. It clinched matters when Lydia said, "Poor little things, they look as if they need someone to love them."

The only outsider at the party was Kerry, and she scarcely seemed like an outsider at all. At long last the twins were beginning to develop individual characters. Beth was glad that this was a family tea party. Not that she was shy, but she enjoyed tradition. Josie had asked for a proper birthday at McDonald's with school friends and paper hats. In the end, she had to settle for the paper hats. Only Jacob quietly declined to wear one.

He had given each of his sisters a silver chain bracelet with their name on: JOSEPHINE MARY and ELIZABETH ANN.

They were delighted. "Our proper names!"

"Yes," said Jacob. "Names are very important."

So his part in their birthday was not entirely negative.

There was one moment when Josie looked his way slyly.

"You're not the only teenager in the family now," she said. "We are ten and that is double figures, so we are teenagers as well."

"No," said Jacob with a smile. He did appreciate being included but he had to stick to the facts. "You aren't. It has to have *teen* in it. So it can't start till you're thirteen."

"What do you think, Dad?" said Beth.

"I've done enough serious thinking for one day," said Steven. "Let's all have a game of Monopoly."

If I land on Park Place, thought Jacob, *I'll get to see Nesta tonight.*

That evening in the computer room, to Jacob's delight, his father decided that they should check up on the Gwynns to see how they were doing.

"I'm feeling a wee bit guilty about putting off going to see them," he said. "There is a side to the argument that says, Give them time to get used to their new situation. Strictly speaking, I could argue that they are no longer entitled to any support from me. But habit dies hard. If they are no longer Ormingatrig, that is something I shall have to get used to."

"Yes, Dad," said Jacob with conviction. "And you really are supposed to keep an eye on them. You never know what they might be getting up to."

"I've a fair idea," said Steven, unfurling the screen above the Brick and tuning in to York.

"Yes?" said Jacob.

"Let's see," said his father, looking at his watch. "It is now nine-thirty. I'd guess they are reading, writing, or watching television."

"They might be out," said Jacob.

"They might be," said Steven absently as he concentrated on getting the view he was seeking.

The screen showed the front of the house in Linden Drive. Gradually, Steven homed in on it till the probe was able to enter the front room. Sure enough, there they were. Matthew was watching television—some program about ancient ruins. At a desk in one corner of the room, Alison was working at something, pen in hand, papers either side of her. From time to time, she looked toward the television screen and made some remark about it.

"She's half-watching and half-working—a bit like your mother!" said Steven.

"Where's Nesta?" said Jacob. He was just beginning to think that landing on Park Place hadn't worked when the door opened and Nesta came in. She took what looked like a schoolbook to her mother, who set aside her own work and gave her full attention to her daughter.

"She's getting help with her homework," said Jacob. Nesta's fine hair fell over her cheek as she looked down at the book. The fingers of her left hand settled on the page, a small, fine hand with tapering fingers. As she turned her head to look at her mother, Jacob saw once more the blue-gray eyes and remembered how they had met his as he looked in from the garden.

"There," said Steven, "what did I tell you? Nothing to see."

"Maybe we should watch a little longer," said Jacob.

"Or maybe I should check on Elgarith," said Steven. "I am never sure that he can manage on his own. The Marseilles situation is always fraught with danger. The shield around him might need intensifying."

CHAPTER 27

The Invitation

To invite Amy to stay at Linden Drive for the half-term holiday was Alison's idea. What she had heard of Amy's efforts to look after Nesta made her think that she would be a good friend for her daughter, perhaps a friend for life. She wanted to have Amy as an ally. She also wanted to make it easier for Nesta to put the Ormingat episode right to the back of her mind.

"It's part of the healing process," she said to Matthew when she broached the subject with him. "We are Earth people now. We must try to make it as if Ormingat had never existed."

"Can you mean that?" said her husband, appalled at the idea. "We can, and probably should, cease to talk about Ormingat, but if I live to be a hundred, I shall never forget that this is not where I truly belong."

He looked at Alison a long time before adding, "The hurt of losing my homeland will never really go away. There is no healing for that."

"It hurts me too," said Alison, "but we had no choice. You must see that. Now we have to be practical—for Nesta's sake, if not for our own. It's over. We were clearly told that we had lost all possibility of returning when our ship left without us. So live for the day, Maffaylie. Or if a day is too long, live for the hour."

Matthew smiled, aware that Alison had unconsciously used his

134

Ormingat name. She was accustomed to hiding her deeper feelings, but occasionally the mask slipped and she gave something away.

"And if the hour is too long, Athelerane?" he whispered, his hand in hers.

"Oh, Matthew," said Alison, shaking her head. "I am still muddled. But time will straighten things out in our mind. If we can't quite manage to be what we now are, we must pretend, and go on pretending. There is nothing else for it."

"I sometimes wonder if our people really are finished with us," said Matthew pensively. "I mean, for all we know they could be keeping an eye on us from somewhere. You'd think they'd be bound to wonder how much we have given away."

"That's pure speculation," said Alison firmly. "Some ideas are best left well alone."

"What did your mom say? Did she say you could come?" said Nesta eagerly.

She had arrived at school before Amy and waited anxiously at the gate for her friend to arrive. Now the two of them were walking into school together and Nesta could hardly wait for Amy's reply.

"She said yes. But she's being very formal about it. She's going to send a card to your mother thanking her for the invitation. I think it's her way of checking up on me, but I don't mind. And it might not be. She likes sending cards to people."

"Well, there's no harm anyway," said Nesta. "It's not as if you were running away or anything."

After she had said this she blushed, recalling how just a week ago she had been a runaway herself. She'd got off very lightly. Mom had taken her back to school on the Tuesday, made excuses for her, and made sure that the episode would be put behind her.

The teachers all knew, of course, but had been asked not to

make any reference to Nesta's absence. Mrs. Powell had already had to deal with the bullying that Nesta had suffered in her first year at the school, and she was by no means certain that this had not been behind the girl's absconding. The Boston story sounded far-fetched to her. But "least said, soonest mended" was an axiom she could go along with.

The two girls reached the cloakroom and sat down on the form beneath the rack, their shoulders resting against the coats.

Amy had made up her mind to say something. "I'd like to tell my mum that you stayed in our garage those three nights."

Nesta looked horrified. "It's all over and done with," she said. "No point in dragging it up now. Why do you want to tell her?"

Amy ran her fingers through her wiry hair and bit her lip before answering.

"I feel rotten about it," she said. "I felt proud at first at getting away with it, but it seems like cheating somehow. Especially when Mum's being so nice about the holiday."

Amy did not tell her friend that her mother had not been so happy at first, but had been persuaded to feel sorry for that "poor girl who ran away because she didn't want to go to America." Mrs. Brown had never been out of England and had never wanted to go abroad. "My own country's good enough for me." Her own country, her own family, her own little world . . . When the police had come looking for Nesta, she readily believed that Amy knew nothing about her friend's whereabouts.

Nesta grasped Amy's arm tightly. "It'll never happen again," she said. "Soon we'll be able to forget it altogether. It wasn't all that serious, was it? Not in the end. I came home and everything was all right—and my mom and dad didn't go to Boston. But if you go telling your mother about it now, it'll just all start up again. Just for me, Amy, please let's pretend it never happened."

"What about when I come to your house for half term?" said

Amy. "Won't your parents be asking questions about me hiding you?"

"No," said Nesta. "That's the best of it. They know all about it. I even made them promise not to split on you. We wiped the slate clean. And we are never to mention it again."

Amy still looked doubtful. Her own code of conduct required everything to be open and aboveboard. One day she would play hockey for the county and she already had the attitude of a true sportswoman. But loyalty ranked high too. To tell might be a breach of her loyalty to Nesta.

"Just as long as you know I'm not happy about it," she said. "But for your sake, I'll keep quiet."

After school on Friday, the twelfth of February, Nesta and Amy boarded the bus to Linden Drive. Amy had a large holdall "packed for the holiday." True it was only a few miles from home, but it felt exciting. It was not quite the same as camping out in the garage at Amy's house, but both girls felt that it would be really good fun.

"My brother lent me his PlayStation," said Amy, "and loads of games."

She already knew that computer games were not part of the Gwynn household: Nesta sometimes complained about her parents not being "with it." So Jack's games machine would be quite a novelty.

"Mom won't let me have a telly in my bedroom," said Nesta, "because she says Mrs. Jolly might be able to hear it and not like the noise. But there's a portable in the kitchen. We can play with it in there."

By the time the bus reached the corner of Linden Drive, they had thought of dozens of things to do in the week's holiday, including the history homework that Mr. Fielder had maliciously set them. There was a list of fifty famous dates to be matched up on a worksheet, going all the way from the Roman invasions to the major events of the twentieth century. "I doubt if you'll want to be gallivanting in this sort of weather," he had said, smiling sardonically. "This'll be a nice little indoor game for you."

Nesta had felt as if he looked especially at her as he rolled out the word *gallivanting*, but that could have been imagination!

It was raining heavily when they got off the bus. Mrs. Gwynn was waiting for them, holding her huge golf umbrella.

CHAPTER 28

Traveling North

On Monday, the fifteenth of February, Steven and Jacob set off on their trip to the North. It was a sensible, properly arranged holiday, father and son off together to visit a computer show in York and then on to another one in Sunderland. That was not even a lie. There really were computer shows scheduled for those venues, and Steven really did intend to look in on them. Lydia was used to her husband's work taking him away from time to time. It now seemed very natural that Jacob should follow in his father's footsteps.

The train left King's Cross Station at ten-thirty in the morning. Father and son settled down in the seats reserved for them. Today they were traveling as far as York. Steven had decided not to go by car. He had no intention of buying anything: the computer shows were no more than a useful pretext.

"The show's on Wednesday," said Steven, "and we'll head for Casselton straight afterward. The Sunderland show is on Friday. We'll look in on that on the way home."

"And in York today," said Jacob, "we'll get to see the Gwynns."

"You're looking forward to that, aren't you?" said his father.

"Yes," said Jacob, "I am. You do realize that I have seen what you have never seen?"

"Oh?"

"I have seen another Ormingatriga face to face, here on Earth, and not just on a screen."

"I hadn't thought of it that way," said Steven. "It will be strange talking to them. Till now, it has been strictly against the rules."

The day was cold but bright. For a while, Jacob looked out the window at the passing fields while Steven read the newspaper. Silence eventually gave birth to thought. Jacob asked again the question his father had failed to answer.

"The communicator said your work had to be finished by the first of March. I asked you why. You never gave me an answer."

Steven folded the newspaper and tucked it into the netting on the seat in front. "I suppose I'd better tell you now," he said. "You have a right to know."

"Well?"

"Remember how I altered the clock on the Gwynns' spaceship?"

"Yes."

"I had to do the same with ours. It was an order and I was inside the ship. Even if I had wanted to disobey, I was in no position to do so. You must understand that."

"Dad," said Jacob irritably, "so far, I understand nothing, though I'm beginning to guess."

"Well, then, to cut a long story short, if that's what you want, our own spaceship is now scheduled to take off on the first of March at two o'clock in the morning."

At first Jacob could not quite grasp what this implied. "Where is the ship meant to be going? How long will it be away?"

He had already seen one short trip, when Patrick Derwent was flown from Edinburgh to Casselton. All sorts of trips were surely possible? Especially for his father, the facilitator, the custodian of the Brick, the manipulator of shields.

"Are you being deliberately stupid?" said Steven with a flash of anger. "I—and you—we are meant to be going to Ormingat. There is no return ticket."

Jacob felt breathless and sat back, just staring down the carriage but not really seeing anything.

"Say something," said Steven. "You know it now. So what do you say?"

"I can't say anything," said Jacob. "I don't know what to say."

"Will it help if I tell you that we aren't going?" said his father with a smile that was more sad than happy. "We can stay here on Earth and let the ship go without us."

"Another ship going into space without passengers?" said Jacob. "That doesn't seem right or fair."

Steven was pensive. Jacob seemed wise beyond his years. Steven felt compelled to be totally honest with him and to try, somehow, to convey some of his own deeper thoughts.

"I know what you mean," he said. "In fact, I know better than you what a failure this is. For two hundred and fifty years, spaceships have traveled to Earth and back. Never till now has a ship returned without its passengers. And now there has been one, and there will be two. The Ormingatriga in me, kept secret but powerful and pulling at my heartstrings, can only see it as dire failure. The system that brought us here is breaking down. Maybe it started with the crash on Walgate Hill. Perhaps it goes further back than that—when Kraylin broke the STI and no means was found to mend it. But I can't be responsible for anybody else. My own failure is my own—just that. I am not part of a pattern."

Jacob saw with alarm that his father's eyes were brimming with tears. "Well, go," he said. "If it is so important, we can both go. I too am Ormingatrig."

"You too are Lydia's son," said Steven. "Would you break her heart?"

Jacob was fourteen and could already see that the world was bigger than Heath Lane. It was even bigger than London.

"I will be leaving someday," he said. "I love my mother, I love her very much, but if necessity says leave, then perhaps I could. And if you must go, then surely I should. It's not easy to think about."

"It is," said Steven grimly. "It is very easy. I have been dishonest with myself till now. There is no way in this universe that I could ever leave your mother. She needs me."

"She might not," said Jacob. "What would happen if you died? She would have to manage without you then."

"If I died," said his father, "then she would not be my responsibility. But while I live and breathe I must look after her."

"She's not a child."

"No," said Steven, "but her whole life revolves round her home and her family. I can't destroy her happiness. She is my waif-soul. She is my Matchgirl standing out in the snow. Don't ask me again what that means. I don't choose to tell you." He squeezed his eyelids together to force back his tears.

Jacob linked his arm through his father's and leant briefly against his shoulder. "So the ship will go home empty?" he said.

"Unless I can find some other passengers to take our place," said Steven in a voice that was deliberately flippant.

"Ormingatrig?"

"They could hardly be anything else!"

The train drew into York Station, on time for once, and Jacob and Steven descended in silence. Hardly a word passed between them as they checked into the hotel where they would be staying for two nights before traveling further north.

In silence they made their way to the bus stop outside the Museum Gardens. It was the second time Jacob had made this trip. He had been looking forward to showing his father the way, to being his guide on a real bus to a real house in a real street. But now much of the exhilaration had gone. Why did life have to be so serious?

Steven put an arm round his shoulders. "It's not all that bad, you know," he said awkwardly. "Even if the ship has to return empty, I'll guide it on its way. I expect they'll even want me to go on working for them. It'll be harder without the communicator. But I can do wonders with the Brick. You know I can. You've seen me."

CHAPTER 29

In York

Despite the cold, Nesta and Amy spent the morning in York, looking round the shops and buying things that were cheap and cheerful. Mainly, it was things to wear; but Nesta managed to find a copper pendant that looked worth far more than she had paid for it, and Amy found a juggling clown to add to her collection.

"It's like being a tourist," she said. "I'm pretending that I don't live here but have just come down from Scotland for a visit. You can be my American friend, come over from the States."

"I think I can manage that," said Nesta with a grin. "We Yanks do so love your historic city. What say we take a trip to the Jorvik Centre?"

"No," said Amy. "That takes time and money. Let's pretend we went there yesterday. Today we're into buying souvenirs for the folks back home."

"Stop!" said Nesta. "You have your 'ain folk' and are 'frae the Highlands.' The 'folks back home' would definitely be mine."

A few stray flakes of snow began to fall. The girls were in Piccadilly, not far from the bus terminus. The bus for home was standing there waiting.

"Let's pack in for the day," said Amy. "That's our bus over there. Let's go home and play Tombi. No sense in getting snowed on!"

*

The snow came to nothing, but the girls were still pleased to be sitting in the kitchen, drinking the warm cup of soup that Alison had given them and getting on with the long-running game of Tombi. They took turns holding the controller, the one without it being an eager, and often mistaken, adviser.

The object of the game was to find the pig bags and capture all the pigs, culminating with the pig boss. In that way, the evil pig magic would be defeated and the game would be over.

Finding the pig bags was practically impossible! Nesta, who had never played on a PlayStation game before, soon began to think that the gamemakers were cheating and that some pig bags simply did not exist.

"Your brother should take it back to the shop," she said. "It doesn't work properly."

"It does," said Amy. "It's just very, very difficult. That's why people go on playing it. Give me the controller now. You've had your ten minutes."

There was a ring at the doorbell. The sound of it carried to the kitchen, but the girls did not even look up from their game. They had no curiosity at all as to who might be waiting on the doorstep.

It was freezing cold. A few flakes of snow had fallen halfheartedly but soon gave up their attempt to whiten the world. Steven and Jacob stood shivering on the doorstep of number 8 Linden Drive. Steven rang the doorbell sharply. Then, after a couple of seconds, he lifted the rapper and brought it down hard twice or thrice.

"Give them time, Dad," said Jacob between shivers. "Their car's in the drive. They're nearly sure to be home."

"Just our luck if they aren't," said Steven sourly.

And at that moment the door opened and Alison stood looking out at them with a certain hostility in her gaze. She did not like the way they had rapped at the door. She had never seen them before and had no idea who they were. The man was probably in his late thirties, sallow-complexioned, with high cheekbones and very dark eyes. The boy, obviously his son, was a younger and slightly fairer version of his father.

"Whatever you're selling," said Alison, "we don't want any."

"We aren't selling anything, *Athelerane*," said Steven softly. "We have come to talk."

Alison drew in her breath sharply, cold breath in the cold north air. The name that Steven had given her was all the identification she needed.

"You are of us?" she said tersely.

Steven nodded.

"Come in," said Alison. "Let us talk inside."

She took their coats and hung them in the hall. As she did so, her thoughts were in turmoil. She could not construe the meaning of this visit. And the man had brought his son.

"Come into the front room," she said. "Matthew is there."

She opened the door.

Matthew looked up from the desk where he had been writing. It was puzzling to see two strangers standing there, a man and a boy. Was there some connection with the university, with Alison's work? The boy looked too young to be an undergraduate. And no one from the university had ever visited before.

"We have visitors, *Maffaylie*," she said. Then he too knew who the visitors were.

"Come in," he said. "Do come in and sit by the fire. It's a horribly cold day."

He ushered them to the sofa. Then he and Alison sat down in the armchairs to either side of them.

"This has never happened before," said Matthew carefully. "It is strictly against the code for us to meet."

"Many things have never happened before," said Steven severely. "You and your family should by now be on the spaceship returning to Ormingat. Your breach of the code is by far the greater."

Jacob gave his father a look of disbelief. Surely he wasn't going to blame these people for doing something he had every intention of doing himself?

"To come straight to the point," said Steven, "we need to know how much damage your defection might have caused."

Matthew looked baffled. "The spaceship shattered the frog," he said weakly, "but there was no real harm done, and nobody any the wiser."

"That is not what I mean," said Steven. "Physical damage is irrelevant. We have to know whether other Earthlings have any clue as to what happened here three weeks ago. We also need to find out what Nesta has told to her friends and to anyone she might have encountered when she ran away. We need to know much more about her meeting with Stella Dalrymple."

"I can answer all of that," said Alison, "but you must not question my daughter. I don't want her to be upset."

"Where is Nesta?" said Steven.

"She's in the kitchen with her friend. They are playing on some sort of computer game."

Steven considered carefully what to say next. It would perhaps be better to have Jacob out of the way. What Steven had in mind would come better from one person, speaking alone. He was also unsure of what his son's reaction might be.

"Jacob enjoys computer games," he said smoothly. "Would you mind very much letting him join your daughter and her friend in the kitchen? He will be discreet. He would never betray our secret."

Jacob was in two minds whether to rebel at being sent out of the room, but his wish to see Nesta overruled whatever adolescent indignation he might have been feeling.

CHAPTER 30

In the Kitchen

"What now?" said Nesta impatiently. "I can't see any sign of a pig bag."

Her turn with the controller was nearly up and to be stuck at this point was very frustrating. Her neck was beginning to feel stiff with looking up at the screen, but she was caught up in the challenge of the game and the novelty of playing it.

"You've only got a minute left," said Amy. "Then it's my turn."

At that moment the kitchen door opened, letting in a shaft of light from the hall. The two girls looked up, startled.

Mrs. Gwynn was standing there with a strange boy by her side. He would, the girls thought, be about their age or a little older.

"This is Jacob," said Nesta's mother with a bright smile. "His father is here to talk business with your dad. So I thought he'd rather be in here with you. He likes computer games."

Jacob smiled apologetically. He had a feeling that his presence was not wanted.

"Nesta's my daughter," said Alison, nodding toward her, "and Amy here is her friend. She's staying over for the half-term holiday. The games machine is hers. I'm sure she'd be pleased to let you join in."

Alison looked up uncomprehendingly at the little figures

jumping across the screen, shrugged her shoulders, and left the room, closing the door behind her.

Jacob stood, looking straight at Nesta and ignoring Amy as if she weren't there. Nesta gazed back at him.

Both girls were seated at the kitchen table, the games machine between them. On a shelf above the bench in front of them was the television set. Amy had the seat nearest the hall door. To her left stood the stranger; to her right was Nesta. She looked from one to the other and had the momentary urge to snap her fingers, so trancelike did the other two seem.

"I think I have met you before," said Nesta, breaking the silence. "I'm sure I know you from somewhere."

Jacob smiled. "That is the nicest thing anyone has ever said to me."

For an instant the two of them looked strangely alike. Jacob's sallow face and dark eyes were so completely different from Nesta's pale skin, and eyes that were gray-blue and fine-lashed, that the resemblance would be hard to explain. But it was there.

Amy, stocky and robust, was the outsider. She heard what was said and, under her breath, she muttered, "Yuck." Jacob to her sounded soppy and insincere. She had no way of knowing that he meant every word he said. He was probably the only boy on the planet who could have uttered such words with complete sincerity.

"Let's get on with the game," said Amy out loud. "If you want to watch, why don't you just sit down?"

Jacob slipped obediently into the vacant chair she had indicated. The girls turned once more toward the screen.

"My turn," said Amy, taking charge of the controller. Nesta handed it over reluctantly and turned her attention once more to the game.

"Now," said Amy, looking intently at the screen, "what are we supposed to do here? There's nothing in this room but bars sticking out from the walls."

"Swing on them?" suggested Nesta.

"That's right," said Jacob. "Swing up to the highest bar—there's a ledge up there with a chest on it. If you jump on the chest, it will open."

Both girls turned on him crossly.

"You've played this game before," said Amy accusingly. "We haven't! So even if you know all the answers, please just keep shtoom! We want to work it out for ourselves. That's the whole point."

"We might need a little bit of help," said Nesta with slightly less hostility, "but it would be best if you waited till we asked."

The clue Jacob had given them worked. They were soon moving on to the next stage, completely engrossed in the game. Jacob found himself in a very familiar situation: he might as well not have been there. He sat silent, hoping against hope that they would ask for his help. They didn't.

The next time the kitchen door opened, it was Steven who looked in.

"Time to go now," he said.

Alison came up behind him. "We really would like you to stay for tea," she said in a tone that showed that the offer had already been made and refused. "It seems so inhospitable to let you leave like this."

"Not at all," said Steven. "We have to be on our way now. But do remember, the possibility is there. All you need do is follow the directions."

Jacob got up from his seat and look hesitantly at Nesta. "Goodbye," he said.

Both girls turned briefly from the screen, murmured, "Goodbye," and immediately returned to their game.

"Why did we have to hurry away?" said Jacob as they walked along the street. "Where are we going next?"

"Back to our hotel," said Steven. "I need to sleep. This afternoon has drained all my nervous energy. Ormingatrig are not meant to meet here on Earth. Even with consent, the rule is hard to break."

Jacob looked at him curiously. What had they talked about? What did his final words to Alison mean?

"There are things you'll have to tell me, Dad," he said.

"There are things I will tell you, but first I must rest."

CHAPTER 31

Things to Tell

Jacob gave his father two hours alone in his room. Then he decided he had waited long enough. He went across the corridor and knocked at his door.

"Bored?" said Steven as he opened the door.

"Very," said Jacob. "It's too late and too dark to go sightseeing."

"I believe there's a ghost tour of the city," said his father with a grin. "We could try that."

"Let me come in," said Jacob, ignoring the inane suggestion. "It's you I want to see, and I want you to fill in some of the details."

Steven opened his door wider and Jacob walked in and sat down on the basket chair. Steven stretched out on his bed, sitting up with his hands behind his head. The only light in the room was the table lamp.

"So what do you want to know?" he said. "Where do I begin?"

Jacob, as usual, was very direct. "What were you talking about to the Gwynns? What did you find out? And what did you mean by telling Mrs. Gwynn that the possibility was there? What were the directions?"

"You need to know?"

"Of course I need to know," said Jacob impatiently. "You made them an offer, didn't you? You offered them our spaceship. That's what it sounded like to me."

151

"And what, my son, leads you to that interesting conclusion?" said Steven loftily. He was a nonsmoker, but for effect he pretended to take from his lips a long cigarette holder and blow nonexistent smoke rings.

"Be serious, Dad," said Jacob. "When you said that the spaceship could return with other Ormingatrig aboard, I thought you were joking. Now I am not so sure. Did you offer them the spaceship?"

"Yes," said Steven, "as a matter of fact, I did."

"What did they say?"

"They were stuffy about it, as if butter wouldn't melt in their mouths. He said it was against all precedents. It had never happened and never should happen. She was only concerned that her daughter should know nothing of it."

"So they refused?"

"They refused," said Steven. "Though, I have to say, Matthew looked thoughtful, even wistful, for a while. Maybe he's having second thoughts now."

"And if he has?" said Jacob.

"Ways and means," said his father, tapping the side of his nose. "Ways and means."

"But it is our spaceship," said Jacob. "It's not theirs. They have no right to it."

"Yes," said Steven, "and it might not even let them in."

"That would be fair enough," said Jacob. "It is our spaceship. If we don't use it, nobody else should."

After all this time he felt affection for the ship. It was a wonderful part of a secret life and he did not want to lose it.

"It won't be our ship after the first of March," Steven pointed out. "It has never really been ours at all. It belongs to Ormingat. That is where it will return. And, all joking apart, it will return empty."

"What if the Gwynns change their mind?"

"They won't. I know they won't," said Steven, but his son seemed to detect an uncertainty in his father's voice.

"But if they do?" he said.

"If they do, they do," said Steven quite harshly. "I don't choose to talk about it anymore. End of subject. Now let's go out and find ourselves a meal. Tomorrow we'll go sightseeing. On Wednesday we'll visit the computer show at the racecourse. Then it's off up north to Belthorp to deal with Stella Dalrymple."

It was a calculated distraction. Jacob was diverted from the Gwynns to this lady who knew too much.

"Did they tell you anything about her?" he said. "The Gwynns, I mean."

"She knows everything," said Steven. "She knows all about Ormingat and the visitors to Earth. She knew even before Nesta went to see her. When that strip of sheepskin found on the wheel of the tanker matched up with the coat on the hospital bed, she realized that the stories Thomas had been telling her for years were true."

"Does anyone else know?"

"To the best of our knowledge, Stella Dalrymple is the only person on Earth who is aware that the planet Ormingat really exists. So she is a problem I shall have to solve."

Next day they went to the Railway Museum and sent a postcard to the twins. There were many to choose from. Jacob decided that his sisters would like the interior of Queen Victoria's carriage, a wonderful, possible Sindy doll scenario!

After looking at all of the trains, old and new, from *Rocket* to *Eurostar*, they took a bumpy ride in the little road train back to the minster. Then, because the day was dry and bright and not too cold, they decided to walk along the promenade beside the Ouse.

"How will you solve the problem of Stella Dalrymple?" Jacob asked, going back to the conversation of the day before. He had learnt long ago that the best way to get information from his father was to ask little, and not too often.

They walked down the slope that led to the river. There were benches and tables outside a riverside inn. Despite the time of year, some customers were sitting drinking out in the open air.

"Sit there," said Steven. "I'll fetch you a Coke—that's if you'd like one?"

"Okay," said Jacob. *I can be patient, Dad, but I still want the answer.*

He sat watching the river. It was not high today—no floods, no heavy rain, no burst banks. It was all very pleasant and peaceful. Steven came back with a Coke for Jacob and a lager for himself.

"Cheers," he said, lifting the glass.

Jacob did not respond.

"Interesting pub," said Steven, deliberately ignoring his son's silence. "Got a measure on the wall showing how high the floods have reached over the years. The Ouse is not always a kindly river."

But at that moment it looked very kindly and sunlight was glinting on the rippling water. It was not warm, but it was certainly pleasant.

"So how will you solve the problem?" said Jacob resolutely, looking absently at the glass of Coke on the table in front of him, not one sip taken out of it yet.

"Stella Dalrymple?" said Steven.

"Who else?"

Steven said nothing, but drank some lager.

"You'll know eventually," he said at length. "It's really too simple to be of any concern to you."

Jacob glowered at him and drank his Coke.

"The day's not as warm as it looks," said Steven after a while. "I'm beginning to feel quite chilly sitting here. Let's go and check how we get to the racecourse tomorrow. Then we'll have dinner at that place we went to last night. It wasn't too bad, was it?"

CHAPTER 32

Belthorp

Rupert Shawcross knew nothing at all about the Ormingatrig who lived in York. And the Ormingatrig knew even less about Rupert. For two hundred and fifty years, no one had penetrated their secrets—till now. So far as they knew, Stella was their one and only risk, admirable in her ability to believe, frightening in her casual giveaway remark.

Rupert did have other work to do besides trying to solve the mystery of "Starlight, perhaps." As usual, sightings of dubious authenticity had been reported in all sorts of places, from Land's End to John o'Groats. Most of them were incredibly stupid: television masts swaying in mist, lights on airplanes, reflections of the full moon in calm water. Some were vaguely mysterious but soon became clear after investigation. This year, at least, Stella's story was the only one that carried any conviction, so Rupert frequently found himself going back to it, and wondering if he could get anywhere near a solution.

"It's half term next week," said Mrs. Ames on Friday morning as Rupert came into the office. "My grandchildren will be on holiday. I think I'll take Thursday and Friday off, if it's all right with you."

Half term, thought Rupert. *Oh, yes—schools on holiday. That's it.*

"Yes," he said affably, "why not? You might as well. There's not much happening here this week."

"So you're getting no further with 'Starlight, perhaps'?" said Mrs. Ames. "Is that file closed?"

"Not yet," said Rupert. "In one way, I've just about given up on it. In another, I can't. It's easily the most promising bit of information we've had. And that woman is definitely hiding something."

"What about the boy?" said Mrs. Ames. "Mickey somebody?"

"Mickey Trent," said Rupert. "Let's see. It's half term. I've a mind to go north and try to have another word with him. Next Monday and Tuesday, before you have your break. I think I'll take the car. My cousin will put me up. So no need for any booking— might be difficult at the holiday."

"Mickey might not be at home," Mrs. Ames pointed out. "He might be away for the week."

"I'll take a chance," said Rupert. "These village kids are probably lucky if they get one holiday a year. His mother's a widow, I think."

"This is very pleasant," said Audrey. "I don't see you for years on end, and then there you are on my doorstep, twice in next to no time!"

"You don't mind, do you?" said Rupert.

"No," said Audrey, "of course not. Though you'd have been stuck if I'd decided to go away for the week."

Audrey had been a teacher at a comprehensive school in Casselton for the past twenty years. It was not the easiest of jobs. Being on holiday and at home was a treat in itself.

"Come into the box," she said with a laconic smile. "I've made up a bed for you in my 'study'—a posh name for the second bedroom."

The bungalow was indeed small, but Audrey managed, despite her gibes, to make it look reasonably spacious.

"Thanks," said Rupert. "That's good of you. I do appreciate it— and at such short notice."

They were soon seated in the living room with the usual northern tea: plates of sandwiches, biscuits, and cakes that could add up to a fair-sized meal.

"Well, now," said Audrey, "can I guess why you are here?"

"Do," said Rupert, biting into a ham and pease pudding sandwich.

"You have some new clue about that missing boy and you are hot in pursuit."

"Not exactly," said Rupert with his usual honesty. "I am just trying to get a bit further with what I already know."

"Tell you something," said Audrey seriously, "I don't think you'll ever find him."

"Why not?" said Rupert sharply. "Do you think he's disappeared off the face of the earth?"

Audrey put her cup down neatly on its saucer. "Listen, Rupert. He doesn't need to have disappeared off the face of the earth. Let me tell you a story, a true one. Last time I was in London, I saw this child sitting on the pavement beside Victoria Station. She couldn't have been more than thirteen or fourteen. I'm a teacher—I should have some clue about how old kids are. She caught my eye and said, 'Gis sumthin forra packit o' crisps, missis.' The voice was unmistakably northern. I stopped and spoke to her. She was from Tyneside. I said, stupidly perhaps, "Why don't you go home to your mam, love? I'm sure she'll be missing you." Then she said sorrowfully, "Yi knaa nowt. A cannit do that." Her eyes brimmed with tears. I gave her some change out of my purse—not a lot, less than I wanted to. But my friend was standing by looking cynical. "She'll only spend it on ciggies," he said, "or something worse." We walked away, but it brought home to me more clearly than any statistic the fact that there are children who disappear and are never found again."

The story made Rupert feel uncomfortable. "I'm not a fraud, Audrey," he said, "so I have to say that there's more to this disappearance than a simple case of a runaway child. Besides, you know the story. You have to admit it is very mysterious."

"So who are you questioning this time?" said Audrey.

"The boy," said Rupert. "Remember, that's what you advised me to do. Seek out Thomas's best friend."

"But you must have questioned him already," said Audrey.

"There's one more fact that's niggling me," said Rupert. "I want to know about the girl who visited Mrs. Dalrymple. That boy took her to Stella's house."

The next day, Rupert went off to Belthorp to see Mickey Trent. He tried the newsagent's first, hoping to waylay him there. It was, after all, a village shop—not inconceivable that Mickey might be hanging around there with his friends again. The frosty reception Mickey had given him on that last occasion was no deterrent to someone as thick-skinned as Rupert Shawcross. But Mickey and his friends were nowhere in sight.

"Did she like the chocolates?" said Sam Swanson with a smile.

Rupert looked at him vacantly, bought the nearest newspaper to hand, and left the shop.

He made his way to Mickey's house and was standing outside, wondering how to approach Mrs. Trent, when the door opened and out she came with Mickey behind her. She stopped to lock up. Mickey saw the prowler and glowered at him.

"Ah, Mrs. Trent," said Rupert, "I was just thinking about you, remembering that little talk we had about Thomas Derwent and his father. They still haven't turned up anywhere, you know. I suppose you're as mystified as the rest of us."

Mrs. Trent looked at him with disapproval. She was too shy and too good mannered to make her feelings known, but this man was becoming a pest.

"I don't think you'll ever find them now. They mustn't want to be found," she said. "There are people like that."

"Mickey might be able to help," said Rupert, plowing on in very heavy soil. "I believe he was talking to a girl who visited Mrs. Dalrymple. She may have told him something."

Mickey came and stood between his mother and the inquisitor. "Look, mister," he said. "It's no use. I'm not going to say anything to you about Thomas or Mrs. Dalrymple or anybody at all. You talk rubbish and your questions are daft."

Jenny Trent blushed at her son's words, though she privately agreed with them. So she made no apology, but simply said, "I'm sorry, Mr. Shawcross, but we'll have to go now. I really don't want to miss the bus."

They hurried away and left Rupert crossly thinking, *They are hiding something. They are all hiding something.* He walked over to the shop again, determined to make one last effort at breaking the silence.

"And you two boys saw Mickey showing this girl the way to Mrs. Dalrymple's house?" he said with an ingratiating smile. Philip and Anthony were busy sorting papers at the side counter.

"What is it you're looking for?" said Sam, coming over to check on this peculiar stranger.

"He wants to know about—" began Anthony in all innocence.

"He's not going to know about anything," said Philip, giving his brother a shove. "We don't know nuffin and we ain't saying nuffin!"

Sam grinned at his son's pseudoaccent. "That's the ticket," he said. "Now, sir, this is a shop. Were you wanting to buy something? Another newspaper perhaps? We do them in all shapes and sizes!"

Rupert left the shop with not another word. He stood at the bus stop seething with irritation.

If only his visit had been made a couple of days later, he might well have had other strangers in his sights. Poor Rupert, with all his earnestness and thoroughness, was destined never to be in the right place at the right time.

CHAPTER 33

A Restless Night

Jacob left his father sitting in the bar of the hotel, talking to another computer buff who had come all the way from Scotland for a conference and would be at the show next day.

"Synchronization's the thing," the man was saying. Jacob hadn't a clue what they were talking about and was glad to go to his own room to settle down for the night.

He drew the curtains to shut out the dark. The room was rather bare, with walls painted an uncomfortable shade of yellow. It was at the back of the building. Outside there was a metal fire escape leading down to a dimly lit courtyard. Nothing to see, nothing to do. There was a TV set in the corner of the room opposite his bed, but Jacob chose not to watch it. Last night he had retired much later, after a nightcap in his father's room and a long, if somewhat empty, talk about the Gwynns. Steven was expert at evading unwelcome questions without even seeming to do so.

Tonight Jacob's one idea was to get straight to sleep, to make morning come more quickly. He skipped a shower, cleaned his teeth, got into his pajamas, and said his prayers: ". . . as it was in the beginning, is now, and ever shall be, world without end. Amen." The church at home might seem like a club to which he did not quite belong, but that special prayer could encompass everything, even Ormingat. So it seemed to Jacob.

He lay on his side, curled up and ready for sleep. But sleep would not come. He had made every effort to relax. He had deliberately missed out on the shower in case it woke him up too much. He should have been tired. But sleep refused to come.

The pillow was too hard.

He thumped it and plumped it, but to no avail.

The room was too dark.

He switched on the bedside lamp.

Then the room was too light.

So he turned onto his back, stretched out, put his hands behind his head, and surrendered to the thoughts that came crowding in. . . .

For a year and a half, Javayl the outsider, child of the broken word, had himself belonged to a very exclusive club. There were just four members: Javayl, Sterekanda, the Brick, and the Cube. Their clubhouse was a spaceship buried in a grave in Highgate Cemetery. It had been the most wonderful time of his life.

For Jacob, losing the spaceship was not a matter of losing the choice of flying to a faraway planet. It was simply losing the spaceship, having his clubhouse pulled down about his ears. This was the dreadful thought that kept sleep at bay. If the Gwynns, by any chance, took their place in the spaceship, it would feel as if they had stolen it. The long-ago entwining had placed something in Jacob's heart that would not go away. Everything else in his life went out of focus. His mother and sisters were blurred and distant. A deep yearning for a faraway place he had never seen, or could even envisage, overwhelmed him. I love Ormingat.

It was after midnight when Steven retired to bed. His room was larger than Jacob's and faced the street, three floors above the ground. From his window he could see a large, railed garden with ornamental trees, leafless for winter. A few cars were still going up and down the hill. But, on the whole, the world was quiet. Steven closed the curtains and prepared for bed.

Last night he had slept from sheer exhaustion. The interview with the Gwynns had taken its toll. The time he had spent parrying all those questions Jacob kept firing at him had demanded too much effort for the time of night. He had been glad to see his son go off to his own room and leave him in peace.

Tonight was different.

He could not sleep at all.

"I always stay here when I'm in York," the man in the bar had said. "The beds are about as comfortable as you'll find anywhere—even at home!"

Tonight the bed in Steven's room felt hard and unyielding. The pillow was too flat. The wool blanket itched through the sheet. Nothing felt right.

At one o'clock he was still awake—awake and worrying.

How was he going to approach Stella Dalrymple?

How would he go about dealing with her?

How would he even get to talk to her?

He could just imagine himself and Jacob knocking at her door. She would open it just a little. What would she see? A man and a teenage boy whom she had never met and knew nothing about. She would hardly be likely to invite them in. They could be anyone, thieves or murderers. She had closed the door on the reporter. She had said just two words and then closed the door.

If we get in, we're all right, Steven thought over and over again, but *we might not even get across the doorstep.*

At breakfast next morning, Jacob and his father were both very tired. They helped themselves to juice and cereal and then sat at a table by the window.

"I couldn't sleep last night," said Jacob. "I kept worrying about the spaceship."

"Hmm," said Steven, and quickly gestured to his son to be silent as the waiter approached with the coffeepot.

"There's nothing to worry about," he went on after the intruder had moved off to another table. "The spaceship will leave in the early hours of the first of March and we shall never see it again."

"That is what I am worried about," said Jacob. "I don't want never to see it again. It's our spaceship. Can we not just keep it and stop it from flying anywhere?"

"You know we can't," said Steven. "I've already explained that to you."

"You could make some sort of arrangement with the Cube," said Jacob. "I know the Brick can be a bit shirty, but the Cube sometimes seems quite friendly. It might understand."

Steven put down his spoon and drops of milk spurted onto the table. "Jacob Bradwell," he said quietly but with deep irritation, "how can you be so—so anthropomorphic? The Brick is a protection module. The Cube is a communicator. They do not possess attitudes!"

"Toast?" said the waiter. "Brown or white?"

"Anything," said Steven impatiently. "It doesn't matter."

The waiter placed a rack with two rounds of each in it on their table and quickly moved away.

"I have my worries too," said Steven. "I don't really know how we are going to deal with Mrs. Dalrymple. So now you know."

Jacob shuddered at the thought of dealing with this woman. He did not know what his father meant. But for the moment he was too tired to ask. There would be time on the train going north.

They helped themselves to cheese and meats and finished breakfast in silence. It was not an ominous silence. It was not even a thoughtful silence. It was, purely and simply, two men too tired to sing a tired song.

"I think we'll skip the computer show," said Steven, "and get an earlier train north. We both need a rest."

CHAPTER 34

Matthew Decides

"Don't even think about it!"

The door had closed on the Bradwells. So far as the Gwynns knew, they were on their way back to wherever they came from. In the kitchen, the girls were still pursuing the elusive pig bags. Matthew and Alison were seated in the green armchairs, facing one another across the hearth.

"I can see you are tempted," Alison went on, "but, please, for all our sakes, don't give it another thought."

Matthew smiled at her weakly, self-deprecatingly. "The idea of actually boarding a ship and returning home has its attractions," he said, "but it goes no further than that. Apart from the fact that Nesta has made it quite clear that she won't go, I don't trust that fellow at all."

"I trust him," said Alison. "He is Ormingatrig and clearly no liar. He is, I believe, even well intentioned. That is what makes him dangerous."

"He's a maverick," said Matthew with unusual vehemence. "He may be all you say he is, but he has no regard for the rules. If we took his place in his ship to journey home, we would be as bad as he is. I know he is likable and friendly, but he has no proper respect for risk. I suppose that's why he's a facilitator and I am just a researcher."

"What do you mean?"

"He lives on a different level from us. He has spent years manipulating things—things and people. He could get himself out of situations that would leave us baffled."

Alison, not for the first time, saw wisdom in Matthew that she often failed to appreciate. She smiled at him affectionately. "I'll go and make the tea," she said.

Nesta and Amy hardly noticed when Alison came into the kitchen. They were deep in the pursuit of a particularly devious purple pig bag.

"We'll have tea in the front room," said Alison. "It's cozier in there. Ready in ten minutes, if you can drag yourselves away from the machine!"

Amy looked up guiltily. "Thank you, Mrs. Gwynn. We'll pack up now. We *have* been playing a long time."

Nesta had control of the game at that point.

"Leave it now, Nesta," said Amy. "We can save it and go back to it later."

"Okay," said Nesta reluctantly. "I suppose so."

The food was set out on the low table in front of the settee. The two girls shared the settee and Alison and Matthew sat in the armchairs again.

"What would you like to do tomorrow?" said Alison gently. "I mean, you don't want to spend your whole holiday slaving over a hot computer game!"

"Well," said Matthew, joining in, "we could all go for a drive. I know the weather's a bit iffy, but we could drive up to Scarborough. If the sea's choppy, we can watch the waves. And I know a nice little café where we can have lunch."

Nesta gave a deep sigh. She felt embarrassed that Amy should see how utterly square her parents were. Recalling things like the karaoke box in the Browns' garage, and thinking of the PlayStation game she was just itching to return to, it seemed to her that there was more than one sense in which her family were aliens. They were seriously out of date.

"Can't we do something more interesting?" she said. "It's not that I'm ungrateful, Dad. But you do come up with some tame ideas!"

"All right," said Matthew a trifle impatiently. "It was only an offer. Where would *you* choose to go?"

Nesta looked speculatively at Amy.

Amy said nothing. She would have been very happy to go and watch the waves crashing against the cliffs.

"We could go down to Sheffield," said Nesta.

"Sheffield?" said Matthew.

"We could have a trip to Meadowhall. There are loads of shops there—and a bowling alley. Suzanne Pearson was there at Christmas and she said it was great. I might get some ideas for my birthday present."

Now seemed the right moment for Matthew to mention another plan that he had been thinking about. It would be better to discuss it in front of Amy so that she would know that, whatever was decided, Nesta was not going to be snatched away to some unwelcome place. Recent experience had taught him to be cautious.

"Yes, honey," he said. "We are not likely to forget it's your birthday in a couple of weeks' time. Thirteen is quite a special age. I'd like us to do something special for the occasion."

"Not a party," said Nesta in mock horror. "Please, not a party!"

"A bit more special than that," said her father.

Alison looked at him, mystified, wondering what he was going to say next.

"What then?" she said.

"Don't you know either, Mom?" said Nesta, looking more interested.

"I haven't a clue!"

"It seems to me," said Matthew, "that on your thirteenth birthday it would be nice for you to see the land of your ancestors. We'll take a trip to America."

Amy gave her friend a worried look, remembering what had happened last time America was on the agenda.

"Why would we want to go to America?" said Nesta tersely.

"To lay a few ghosts," said Matthew. "You need a past and a future. Look at Amy—she knows where she belongs. Her grandmother lives near Pickering, and she has cousins in Beverley. I can't give you that, honey—much as I would like to. But I can let you see the Statue of Liberty. I can let you know where your family is from."

Amy's family had been discussed when she first arrived, bringing with her not only the PlayStation game, but also an invitation for Nesta to spend a week with her at her grandmother's farmhouse in the summer holidays. The cousins from Beverley were going to be there.

"Are you sure?" said Alison.

Matthew looked at her wistfully. "I am completely sure," he said.

Amy looked at Nesta hopefully. What Mr. Gwynn said sounded so reasonable. There was no question of helping Nesta to hide out anywhere ever again.

"I think I'd like that," said Nesta very deliberately. "Yes. I'm sure I would."

"Settled then," said Matthew. "I'll make arrangements tomorrow."

"What about school?" said Nesta. "We'll be back at school by then."

"I'll see Mrs. Powell," said Matthew. "It will only be for one week. We won't be staying away indefinitely."

*

"What was all that about?" said Alison after tea was over and the girls had left the room.

"It is, if you like to think of it this way, a sort of experiment. We shall never return to Ormingat. We are here on this Earth for the rest of our lives. What I am suggesting is making our lives as real as possible. Virtual reality is not enough. We are supposed to be Americans, emigrants from Boston. But that's not just a cover story anymore. It's as near as we can get to having roots here on Earth."

"It could go wrong," said Alison. "It could all break down."

"That's where my faith is stronger than yours," said Matthew. "It could go wrong, but I am going to make sure that it won't."

A momentary doubt crossed Alison's mind. But she dismissed it as not just unworthy, but totally impossible.

CHAPTER 35

Seeing Stella

Steven sat on Councillor Philbin's park bench on the Green in Belthorp. Diagonally across from him, on the other side of the square that included the Green and a broad, cobbled roadway, was the row of Merrivale cottages where Stella Dalrymple lived. It was just after two o'clock on a bright but chilly Thursday afternoon.

Jacob was already on the Merrivale side of the Green, making his way toward Mrs. Dalrymple's house, rehearsing over and over again what he was meant to say.

"Yes?" said Stella when she opened the door to him. Before her was a boy of about thirteen or fourteen. He was not someone she had ever seen before. "What is it?"

"We need to talk to you," said Jacob. "My father and I have things we need to tell you about."

Stella looked at him suspiciously. "Where is your father?" she asked.

Jacob pointed across the Green to the seat where Steven was sitting.

"Why has he not come to the door with you, if he has something to say?" said Stella, cautiously placing one foot behind the door. The boy did not look strong enough to force an entry, but one never knew.

"He thinks you won't talk to a man and a boy who just knock

at your door without any introduction. We could be thieves or murderers."

"He's probably right," said Stella with a smile. This must be the oddest conversation she had ever had on her doorstep. "Are you going to tell me what it is you're after before I close the door and go back to my ironing?"

"We know where Thomas and his father are," said Jacob.

"In that case," said Stella very firmly, "you should tell the police."

"They wouldn't believe us," said Jacob. "Besides, we just want you to know that they are safe. And Nesta's safe too. We saw her with her family in York."

Stella's hand dropped from the side of the door. "Nesta!" she said in a voice little higher than a hoarse whisper. The Nesta connection was surely unknown to Rupert Shawcross or any of his people. This boy and his father, whoever they might be, were surely genuine—whatever *genuine* might mean in this ever more baffling context. She stood for some seconds and just stared at the boy.

Then, being Stella, she could not stay fazed for long. She drew a deep breath, opened the door wider, and waved toward the man on the Green.

"You'd better come in," she said to the boy. "Tell your father to come quickly. The fewer who see you, the better."

Stella did not immediately make her visitors welcome. They could not be kept standing outside—that was clear; but inside, she kept them in the little hall and asked very directly why they had come to see her.

"I don't know why I should be pestered in this way," she said. "I have not asked for your attention."

"I know," said Steven in a soft, charming voice, "and all I can do is apologize. Your mistake was in talking to that reporter, you know."

"Yes," said Stella with a sigh. "Such a clever thing to say—

'Starlight, perhaps.' It rolled off my tongue before I had the chance to catch it. I knew as soon as I said it that it was the wrong thing to say. But I never, ever expected the consequences."

She looked from father to son and wondered what might come out of this visit. Neither of them appeared in any way threatening. Stella had a sense of the muddle they had all got themselves into.

"You know everything, I assume," she continued. "Nesta was here, looking for help. She was so desperate not to be taken away from Earth. Before she came, and after, I had visits from an investigator hoping to find out whether my neighbors came from outer space. He missed you by just two days. Thank goodness he did! Where will it end?"

As she talked, she warmed to them and felt that they were all on the same side.

"You'd better come right in and sit down," she said. "I'll make tea and we can talk."

Steven smiled as they followed her into the living room. The hardest thing had been achieved: they had acquired her trust. The rest should be easy.

"Now," said Stella as they sat by her fireside, "what have you to tell me? Where are Thomas and Patrick now?"

The fire, as usual in this cold season, was burning brightly in the hearth.

"They are miles and miles above Earth, on their way to the home planet," said Steven. "They are perfectly safe. It is a journey that has been accomplished many times before."

"Many times?"

"By different travelers over the past three centuries."

Jacob looked startled. Why was his father telling this Earthling so much?

There followed a long and very deliberate silence. Stella was trapped in it.

"*Look at the logs burning in the fire,*" said Steven softly when he could see that she was calmly waiting for him to speak. "Look at them, Stella. See how the flames lick the wood. See the sparks and listen to the crackling of the wood."

Stella gazed obediently into the fire, her hands folded in her lap.

"Look at the logs burning in the fire, the logs in the fire burning," said Steven, his voice growing ever softer. It was not straightforward earthly hypnotic suggestion. The power behind it was much stronger.

"Your memories of Patrick and Thomas are fading," Steven murmured. "You knew them, you loved them, and they moved away. Keep the love, but lose the knowledge that should never have been yours."

It did not sound like a voice speaking. There was an abstracted, alien ring to it that made it somehow inescapable.

The words were intended for the heart rather than the head. Jacob could not make them out at all. They were not meant for him. But he guessed what was happening. So that was how Stella Dalrymple would be "dealt with"—the dangerous knowledge was being cauterized from her memory.

"When we leave, you will forget that we have ever been here. Seconds after we have closed the door, it will be as if we had never crossed your threshold at all."

Stella turned away from the fire. She shook her head sharply as if to clear it.

"You can't do this to me," she said, looking Steven straight in the eye. "There is no way on this earth that you can deprive me of my memories. I won't let you."

It was Steven's turn to look startled. He had used the power of Ormingat, power of great potency, and it had not worked. He had risked giving Stella more details because he had been so sure he could erase everything.

"I am not a good hypnotic subject," said Stella icily.

"I—I am not using hypnosis, not Earth hypnosis," stumbled Steven. "All I am doing is restoring your memory to full normality. You are meant to remember only those things you know to be possible."

"Thank you, but no thank you," said Stella indignantly. "What will you do if I won't forget?"

Jacob wondered about this. The hypnosis, or whatever it was, had seemed a promising, kindly way of tackling the problem. It had not worked. Now he was afraid that something sinister was about to happen. Surely that was not the way of Ormingat, the peaceful planet? He looked expectantly at his father.

Steven was totally nonplussed.

He had done much harder things than this. It amazed him that it had not worked. There had been a hypnotic element to the treatment, but he had used mind-fencing to induce a sense of irrelevancy. It had been effective on so many other occasions. The subject neither forgot nor remembered forbidden facts—he or she simply ignored them. So why did it not work on Stella?

Not for a moment did Stella fear Steven. "My mind belongs to me," she said, when he was clearly at a loss for words. "While I live, whatever is in my memory stays there, or is displaced because something more important comes along. Could there be anything more important than my love for Thomas and his father? Could there be anything more memorable than our meeting here today?"

"So what shall I do?" said Steven helplessly. "I am meant to protect my planet from discovery."

"Learn what your planet's people have clearly failed to learn so far," said Stella.

"Which is?"

"That there are on this Earth people worthy of trust. When I said those stupid words to that reporter, I didn't realize I was betraying anybody. Now I know better. The secret of Ormingat is under lock and key in my heart. I will never, ever betray you."

"That means you become the protector," said Steven tentatively.

"And you must be the one to forget," said Stella in a firm voice. "When you leave my house today, you must forget all about me.

Go back to your home on Earth—for I take it you have one—and never give me another thought. When you return to Ormingat, make no mention of me there."

"I'm not returning to Ormingat," said Steven, drawn to confide in Stella. "My wife is an Earthling. My children were born here. I could choose to leave them—others must have so chosen in our long history—but I will not make that choice."

It was Stella who noticed the woebegone expression on Jacob's face. She leant toward him and held his hand. "That makes you sad?" she said.

She looked into his dark eyes and saw the depth of his misery.

"I want to keep our spaceship," said Jacob. "I want to be who I am when I am there. It is so much less lonely."

Stella could not quite follow the words, but she understood the sentiment. Someone with less sensitivity might have tried to probe the loneliness. Not Stella. She turned his hand palm upward as if she could tell his fortune. Then she said gently, "It is hard to be lonely. I do understand."

She walked with them to the bus stop and stood till the bus came down from Medfield on its way to the station. It was midafternoon and there were no other passengers either boarding or alighting. That at least was a relief.

"Take care," said Stella as her visitors got on the bus, "and remember what I said about forgetting!"

"We can't just forget, though, can we?" said Jacob when they were seated on the bus. "We have to report back."

Steven smiled enigmatically. "I don't know yet," he said. "There are details we might just fail to remember. There is no need to report at all before the first of March."

"But—" said Jacob, beginning to protest.

"Say no more," said his father. "Let's just enjoy the rest of the holiday. We've done all we can for Ormingat."

174

CHAPTER 36

At Home

"Did you see anything interesting?" said Lydia.

Steven and Jacob had just sat down after arriving back from their "holiday." Their bags were still in the hall, their coats draped over the banister. Tidiness would take a little longer. . . .

At first, Steven was not sure what Lydia meant, such is the power of a guilty conscience, and then he remembered the computer shows they were supposed to have attended.

"We didn't go to the shows," said Steven with complete honesty. "We just rambled round sightseeing instead."

"Good," said Lydia. "You needed a rest from computers. I hoped it wouldn't just be a busman's holiday."

"But I had better check the system, now we are back," said Steven hastily.

It was now two o'clock in the afternoon. "Tea first? Something to eat?" said Lydia.

"Tea later," said Steven with a smile.

Lydia shook her head in mock despair. There was never any point in arguing.

Jacob, as ever, followed his father out of the room.

They ascended the two flights of stairs to the computer room almost at a run. When they got inside, they were rewarded by the sight of the purple button on the lower right-hand corner of the Brick flashing like fury.

"I'm needed," said Steven. "Urgently!"

He sat down quickly at his desk and unfurled the screen above the Brick. There in front of him was not a message but a picture. On a mountainside a woman climber was swinging dizzily out into space from a rope that was so frayed that any second it would break.

"Tollerneek!" said Steven. "In trouble again!"

This time his exasperation was friendly, not the usual bear-with-a-sore-head variety. Truth to tell, he felt pleased to be wanted.

Then suddenly on screen a shield of blue light surrounded the climber and the frayed rope was replaited in an instant.

"I didn't do that!" said Steven, baffled.

Jacob was sitting beside him, watching everything. "Maybe they're training someone else to do your job," he said. "Maybe there's already another Brick somewhere."

"Nonsense," said Steven crossly. "It will simply be emergency cover. They knew I was away and they did not know exactly when I would be back."

"But that still means that someone has another Brick somewhere."

"Of course they have," said Steven. "I am not responsible for the whole world. I don't do Greece, for example. Probably my Greek counterpart has been called in."

The screen blanked out. Steven waited for a message, but none came. Thoughts of being made redundant before his projected return to Ormingat began to trouble him.

"I'll have to check on them all," he said. "I'll have to see what has been happening in my absence."

"All?"

"All thirty," Steven snapped, not looking at his son but keeping his eyes fixed on the screen and his fingers playing nervously across the keyboard. "I am responsible for thirty Ormingatrig in countries from Spain to Lapland. Now leave me alone to get on with my work."

"But—" Jacob began.

"No buts," said Steven, raising his voice. "Get out of my room and let me get on with my job. This is important."

Jacob could not believe his ears. Never, ever had he been spoken to like this. He got up from the stool and walked very stiffly to the door, his head held high. His father did not even notice him opening the door and closing it behind him. His eyes were fixed on the machine, his own special machine in which he was surely the ultimate expert.

Jacob ran down the stairs, grabbed his coat from the newel post, and left the house. Lydia heard the door crash and hurried to see who was coming or going. She opened the door, but by that time Jacob had turned the corner and was out of sight.

It was not until an hour later that Steven came down from the computer room. Eleven of his subjects had received help of varying degrees within the past few days. The other Brick, wherever it was, had been spectacularly active. Steven felt he had cause to worry. He gave no thought to Jacob till he came face to face with Lydia.

"Someone went out," she said. "It wasn't the twins—they're out already. I thought it might be you."

Steven flushed. He took his own coat from the banister, preparing to hang it in its proper place when he realized that Jacob's coat was not there beside it.

"It must have been Jacob going out," he said apprehensively.

"But he's had nothing to eat yet," said Lydia. "And where would he be going?"

Steven looked even more uncomfortable. He found it hard to look Lydia in the eye. She could be so uncannily perceptive.

177

"Maybe he went for a walk," he said. "Maybe he wanted to clear his head."

"I didn't know his head was unclear," said Lydia suspiciously.

"We had a bit of an argument," Steven confessed. "I must have been abrupt with him. I'd better go after him."

"You won't know where to go. You don't know what direction he's gone in."

"I think I might," said Steven. "I'll give it a try anyway. If he gets back before I do, don't let him come out looking for me."

He pulled on his coat and hurried out into the street.

CHAPTER 37

Highgate Cemetery on Saturday Afternoon

When Jacob left the house, he turned straight in the direction of the cemetery. There was not much he could do there but draw near to what he now felt was his second home. It would be impossible on a bright Saturday afternoon to contemplate entering the spaceship, but he could at least be near to where it was. He could stand by the railings and talk to it.

He hurried along Chester Road. It was not as busy as a city street, but there were a few people coming and going on the pavements. Cars passed up and down the road. He even saw a couple of boys he knew from school, but they did not notice him, of course. If he had wanted to speak to, say, Jimmy Pullman, who was in his class at school and whom he saw dragging a skinny dog along on a lead, he would have had to go up to him and deliberately attract his attention. Then Jimmy would have had a word or two with him before moving on. Jacob was not invisible. He was just so unimportant that nobody wanted to know him. That was what years of being shielded had done for him.

The school stood stern and silent as he passed it. On the other side of the road the lower cemetery gates, as always, were locked. A man with a sack on his back paused beside Holly Village to take out a sheaf of leaflets. Jacob passed him and crossed over into Swains Lane.

Here it was even quieter. The street by the cemetery was still bathed in sunlight, but it felt much colder. Jacob walked up the hill, not stopping till he reached the obelisk. He held on to the rusty railings with both hands and peered through at THE GRAVE OF WILLIAM FRIESE-GREENE, THE INVENTOR OF KINEMATOGRAPHY. From a short distance, an angel on another grave appeared to be watching over it. The whole place held a feeling of solidarity. In the cemetery that housed Karl Marx, the dead seemed appropriately united.

This was the way to the spaceship. It would have been possible to approach the grave from inside the cemetery, but at dusk the upper gates were also locked. So an approach through the cemetery had never been practical. Besides, the Friese-Greene obelisk was much nearer to this railing than it was to any gate.

All Jacob needed was some way to make contact with the ground at the base of the obelisk. He found himself idly thinking of how he would manage it. A coat hanger should do: untwist it and turn it into a length of wire long enough to reach the soil. Then, when that contact was made, there would be a rush of air and the Ormingatrig, whose vibrations must be recognized by the ship's sensors, would be drawn down into what to humans would seem to be an inconceivable underworld.

After all, his father's folding ruler was just such another improvisation. A coat hanger would be easier to get hold of than another old-fashioned ruler. He felt sure it would work. He would like to have entered the ship alone and put his case directly for changing the leaving plan. But it would have to be after dark—it had always been after dark—and that would present problems. Neither his father nor his mother would let him leave the house without at least asking where he was going and when he expected to be back.

Jacob went on looking at the spot where the spaceship was hidden. He thought of the Cube that at times was so demanding, but at other times could seem so sympathetic. He looked round to check that no one was near enough to overhear him, then leant closer to the railings so that the rusty metal was touching his cheek. If this was the best he could do, then he must do it.

"Please do not let me lose you," he whispered. "Please ask them to let you stay."

He had no idea who "they" might be, except that his intellect told him that somewhere beyond this Earth there must be those in charge of all the expeditions who might be able to give, or rescind, the orders.

A few weeds were caught by a light breeze, something scuttled through the undergrowth, but otherwise there was nothing that could be interpreted as an answer. Jacob felt the need to put his case more strongly. He held on to the railings tightly and whispered down into the earth, "I have been so unhappy till now, always feeling left out and unwanted. Please want me. Please stay here for my sake."

He must have stood in the same position for nearly an hour, unnoticed by passersby, of whom, in any case, there were not too many at this spot.

Then he gave a jump as a hand gripped his shoulder.

"I am sorry, *Javayl ban*, truly sorry."

Jacob turned round to see his father standing there.

"I should not have been so rude to you," said Steven. "It was very wrong of me and I am sorry."

"And I shouldn't have run off like that," said Jacob, appreciating the apology. "I got upset too easily. I know you were worried. I know you didn't mean it."

"So, friends again?" said Steven, proffering an open palm.

"Friends again," said Jacob, putting out his own palm to meet his father's. A passerby saw the gesture and recognized a family reconciliation. She smiled at them benignly. Steven had no cloak around him and could be seen clearly. The woman who smiled wondered where she had seen him before. Was he a TV star, perhaps, or a footballer?

"I think we had better be on our way now," said Steven. "Your mother will be worried."

On the way home, Steven explained what he had been doing and told Jacob of his findings. It seemed the best way to make up for his earlier sharpness.

"So," he finished, "you were right. There is another Brick, and it looks as if they are grooming someone else to take my place. In due course, they will find out how hard that is!"

"Well, what do we do now?" said Jacob.

"We just wait," said his father. "There is nothing else we can do."

CHAPTER 38

Like a Great Voice Calling

It is not the loudness of the voice. Voices can speak in a faint whisper and still insist upon being heard.

There was a week to go before the spaceship lodged at the base of the Friese-Greene obelisk would leap from the soil and jet out into space. Steven knew that his decision to remain behind would not be accepted as fait accompli till the deed was truly done.

After two days of justifiable sulking, he went to the computer room to check the Brick. Curiosity is a strong motivation. It was Tuesday teatime. Jacob had not yet come in from school. So the coast, as Steven saw it, was clear.

He opened the door for the first time that week.

He looked defiantly at the Brick.

What he saw was not quite what he had expected.

The purple button was flashing, not urgently but intermittently like Morse code. It seemed almost gentle, except that machines do not have attitudes. *Will you, won't you, will you, won't you, will you join the dance?*

Steven slid into his seat and made his presence known. Immediately the screen unfurled and displayed a terse notice.

COME TO THE SPACESHIP.

Then what?

Steven had to think hard what to conceal and what to reveal. He did not want to admit that he had no intention of returning to Ormingat. With only six days to go, it would be a risk to enter the ship and hope to leave, even using deception, which he was not very good at anyway.

He decided that to talk to the machine represented a greater hazard than to type in a reply. Carefully he typed the words:

TOO SOON.

There was no reply. When Steven's words scrolled off the screen, they were replaced by the original message:

COME TO THE SPACESHIP.

"Maybe we should go," said Jacob.

Steven jumped, startled. He had not heard his son come into the room behind him. "Go?" he said rapidly. "Go where?"

"Go to the spaceship," said Jacob. "Tell the truth and ask for the ship to remain on Earth, and explain to the Cube that you want to continue your work here."

"No," said Steven, harshly yanking on the lever to sever communications and sharply scrolling the screen down into place. "Leave it."

"But—" began Jacob.

"No buts," said Steven. "I don't want to talk about it."

"Someone might need you," said Jacob, trying another tack.

That was a tempting suggestion. Steven liked to be needed. The new facilitator, whoever that might be, would not be as proficient. *If I can prove that I am irreplaceable, concessions will be made.*

"Leave me," he said to his son, and then softened enough to say, "You are right. I should do some checking. But leave me now. This is the boring bit, and you know it takes a lot of concentration."

Reluctantly, Jacob left the room, turning as he went to say, "That ship is ours, *Sterekanda mesht*. Make sure they understand."

In the days that followed, Steven would not meet Jacob's eye. His whole manner forbade questioning. He mind-fenced the subject to the best of his ability; but his experience with Stella Dalrymple had taught him that a determined personality is not susceptible to mind-fencing, especially when some important concept is at stake. The computer room was kept locked and he decided not to enter it again until the deadline had passed.

Jacob found himself forced into silence, but he knew every twist and turn of his father's thinking. Clearly, he had failed to put forward a satisfactory argument for continuing his work here on Earth. Now he was determined to block it all out.

A phone call from the insurance company was answered with the excuse that work on their system would have to be suspended for a day or two because the computer terminal was temporarily inaccessible.

"It is a very small glitch," said Steven smoothly. "Tell Anton that everything will be back online next week."

Wednesday passed, and Thursday. The voice of Ormingat kept on whispering to both its sons. One was determined to shut it out; the other was simply reduced to silent misery.

On Friday night, the whispering increased. Jacob was more disturbed than ever. Floorboards all over the house seemed to be creaking. The central heating took longer than usual to settle down for the night. The curtains at his window shuffled with a draft he had never been aware of before.

Come to the spaceship, said the voice inside his head. *Come now. Come quickly.*

That was more easily said than done. Come where? Come how? He eventually slept, but fitfully, and his sleep was filled with unruly dreams.

Then, in the middle of the night, he came fully awake and

realized that he had forgotten to clean his teeth. The taste in his mouth was unpleasant. He welcomed the excuse to get out of bed, to perform a simple everyday task.

He watched himself in the bathroom mirror, scrubbing his teeth, up and down, backward and forward, then up and down again. *Come to the spaceship.* He rinsed his mouth and put the toothbrush back into the rack.

He walked back to his bedroom, passing his parents' room on the way, slightly dawdling, hoping that his father would come out and see him there. The bedroom door opened. It was Lydia.

"I forgot to clean my teeth, Mum," said Jacob quickly.

"So that was the noise I heard," said Lydia. "Do settle down to sleep now. You don't want to waken the rest of the house!"

Steven too had unease inside his soul. But he knew how to recognize the silent sound that managed to seem like a great voice calling. It was the voice of Ormingat, using telepathy to speak to its recalcitrant son. *You have a debt to Javayl.*

On Saturday morning, Lydia rose early, but Steven stayed in bed with the blankets over his ears as if to shut out the sound of the Sirens. The messages that came from Ormingat were sweet and tempting. His human mind might have little recollection of the place to which he truly belonged, but deep inside, he knew. And he cared. He even felt himself assessing the possibilities. He could safely leave the twins to their life on Earth. Much as he loved them, he knew that they would manage without him. He could gladly take Jacob with him into space, and Jacob would be glad to go. But there was no way this side of paradise that he could ever part from Lydia.

"Kerry says we can have a rabbit, Dad," said Josie, "to keep in the back garden."

"We don't know anything about keeping a rabbit," said Steven. "You don't just feed them, you know. I'm quite sure of that.

Would you have to take them to the park for a walk? Do you have to get a rabbit collar and lead?"

Beth was not quite sure whether he meant it or not. She had never seen anyone taking a rabbit for a walk, but it was possible. She looked questioningly at her sister.

"Of course not," said Josie. "You just let them have little runs round the yard and the garden. They're really sweet. And they eat lettuce and carrots."

"Where do they—if you will excuse the word—poo?" said Steven, smiling mischievously. "Do they start off in nappies?"

"Dad," said Josie exasperatedly, "you know they don't. You have to get a hutch at the pet shop. And you have to clean up after them. But they're not very dirty, not like cats and dogs. Their droppings are really quite small, Kerry says."

"Ah-hah," said their father, "so you get this smelly hutch that needs mucking out, like one of the labors of Hercules."

"Stop tormenting them," said Lydia with a laugh. "Your father will go and get you a hutch this afternoon—but you will have to do all the mucking out yourself. And rabbits are not allowed inside the house. If that's clear, I'm sure we'll all get along nicely."

It was Steven who received the hugs and the thanks, but Lydia did not mind.

Jacob stood watching in silence.

On Sunday, while the family were at church, Jacob safely with them, Steven broke his resolve to stay away from the Brick. Alone in the house, he found it difficult to resist checking it just once more. He went into the computer room and unscrolled the screen.

IT IS IMPERATIVE THAT YOU COME NOW.

Steven did not sit down at the table. Nor did he pull the lever that would allow him to speak directly to the Brick. He just leant over the keyboard and typed the words:

187

WHAT YOU ASK IS IMPOSSIBLE.

He left the room again and locked the door.

When the family returned from church, Jacob gave his father a look that clearly expressed suspicion. Steven said nothing and turned toward his daughters, who were in their usual state of high excitement. The hutch was already in the garden, tucked between the shed and the back fence.

"And today we take delivery of the rabbit," he said to the girls. "What shall you call her?"

"It's a him," said Josie.

"And his name's Bob," said Beth. "That's short for Bobtail."

CHAPTER 39

Who Goes Home?

Sunday evening was slow.

Despite Lydia's earlier decree, the hutch and the rabbit were brought into the kitchen because the wind was blowing a gale, and "He is such a little rabbit and he's sure to be frightened." So Josie and Beth sat there with him for company.

Jacob was alone in the dining room, huddled over his history homework, sketching in some detail an early combustion engine. He had a pretty good idea how it worked, which could never be said of the spaceship buried in Highgate Cemetery! He sighed as the thought of the ship pressed on his mind, distracting his attention. Would it really go? Would he never see it again?

Come to the spaceship, Javayl ban.

The voice was more than ever a tiny whisper, unreal but not quite dismissible.

Lydia and Steven were in the front room, deep in armchairs, watching the television in companionable silence. To Steven also the voice was whispering.

Come to the spaceship, breaker of rules. Time is passing. Soon will it be too late.

Steven turned up the sound on the set. It was a program about pyramids in ancient Egypt.

"Is that not a bit loud?" said Lydia, looking up from her sewing.

"Sorry," said Steven, adjusting the sound again. "I didn't mean to turn it up so far."

"They can tell you anything, you know," said Lydia. "The only thing we really know about the pyramids is that they are there. The rest is scholarly speculation."

Steven smiled. "Do you believe in Julius Caesar?" he said playfully.

"Probably not," said Lydia, making a face at him. "Would you like a cup of tea? Than which there is nothing more real!"

To be alone did not suit him at that moment. He followed her into the kitchen and bent down in the corner where the twins were sitting. Then he talked seriously to the rabbit. "There is more to life than lettuce, ol' Bob," he said. "There are carrots and peas and big broad beans. And, glory of glories, there are also bright red radishes!"

The twins listened to him and giggled.

At eleven-thirty Lydia went up to bed, leaving her husband alone watching the television beside the fire in the dimly lit room.

"I'll not be long," he said. "I'll just see the end of this, and then there are one or two things I want to do."

When Lydia left the room, the voice became more insistent, as Steven had known it would.

One hour and the doors will seal. One hour and then nothing more.

Steven turned off the television and went into the kitchen to check that the rabbit was still securely hutched and that all the doors were locked.

Fifty minutes, Sterekanda ban. Bring Javayl. Come now. It is not too late.

The voice was kindly, motherly, friendly. It sounded as if something behind the whispering would deeply care if its instructions were ignored. That was the worst of it. Everyday speech gives a choice of evils: to be caught between the devil and the deep blue sea, a rock and a hard place, Scylla and Charybdis. But Steven's dilemma was to choose between two goods. The waif-soul had to win, but that did not make the loss of Ormingat any more bearable.

So Steven made up his mind to talk to the Brick, to explain the dilemma. As he passed Jacob's door he almost knocked and asked him to join him. Then, that seemed unwise. So instead he made one last effort at mind-fencing.

"Sleep, my son," he said. "By morning it will all be over."

When he entered the computer room, all was as it had ever been. The screen was unscrolled and there, frozen, were the words of command:

IT IS IMPERATIVE THAT YOU COME NOW.

Steven sat down at the desk and switched on the lever that allowed him to speak.

"I am sorry," he said. "I am very, very sorry. I must stay here on Earth with my wife, who needs me, and whose happiness is mine. I do not know how much of this you can hear and understand. I never realized till now just how little I know. I feel there is love for me in Ormingat, and sadness. Please, you who are sad, forgive me. Please, you who love me, know that I feel and cherish your love."

He rested his hands on his arms and wept.

The time passed.

Suddenly, Steven was aware that something was happening above his head, on the screen. He looked up and there was, not the scroll, but a view of Highgate Cemetery in lamplit darkness.

He was aware that something had happened, but he did not know what it was.

Then, at the bottom of the image of the churchyard, like graffiti on the crumbling bricks, appeared the words:

THE DOORS ARE CLOSED BUT THE SHIP IS NOT EMPTY.

Steven gasped. What was happening? What could be happening? The Gwynns!

Had the Gwynns taken him up on his offer? Were they now inside the spaceship? He had told them enough to make it possible. But that girl of theirs did not want to go. Even her mother had seemed reluctant to consider his suggestion. Had Matthew entered the ship alone?

There was only one thing to do. Watch and wait. In less than two hours the ship would leave Earth. The Brick was not responding to him as in former days, but there were clearly things it wanted him to know. Perhaps all was not lost. The Brick could be restored to him and he and Jacob could work with it again.

There is another nuance to the meaning of *Sterekanda*. The rulebreaker was also the one-who-lives-in-hope. Why else would he break the rules?

CHAPTER 40

The Accidental Traveler

No one noticed the boy in blue pajamas haring along the roads of North London in the half hour before midnight.

Jacob might have been sleepwalking. There he was, late at night, running as if his life depended upon it. In his hand he was carrying a thin metal coat hanger, the sort that comes from the dry cleaner's. There were cars passing, and a few pedestrians, but no one noticed him because no one ever did.

The decision to make one last effort to prevail upon the Cube to allow the spaceship to remain on Earth had come to him so suddenly that there seemed no time to dress or wrap up warm, or do anything but run. He knew, of course, that he would not be noticed. On this occasion, it would work to his advantage.

He did not stop or even pause for breath till he reached precisely the right spot along the railings of Highgate Cemetery.

At this hour the place was silent as the grave. Memorials were dark, etched against a lesser darkness. Jacob peered in at the home of the dead, but he did not shudder and no ghost, imaginary or real, came between him and his fixed purpose. William Friese-Greene, master of a different sort of illusion, lay peacefully sleeping, totally unaware of anyone or anything in the world outside.

Jacob painstakingly straightened out the wire of the coat hanger and then pushed up against the railings of the cemetery. In his right hand he held the length of metal. It lacked the rigidity of the folded ruler, but it would be of adequate length. All he needed to do was to put his arm through the railings and hold on to the end of the wire.

It might not work.

He fished round till he could feel the marble of the pediment beneath the obelisk. Then, pulling back an inch or two, he thought he should be in the right place. He had watched very carefully as his father maneuvered the ruler. He squeezed hard against the railing and prodded the wire into the soil. It would not go far, but it did not need to go far. Would it accept Jacob as Ormingatrig? Would it draw him in?

Gladly, willingly, quickly!

The spaceship had been expecting passengers for two days and nights. The final hour was close at hand.

You are late, Javayl, but you are welcome.

These were the first words Jacob heard as he tumbled into the ship. He sat himself upright on the sofa and gazed up at the Cube.

Sterekanda is awaited.

Jacob wondered what to say. Then, remembering what his father had told him of the machine's oblique manner of communication, he made up his mind to say what he had intended to say before he entered the ship.

"I have come to beg you to stay on Earth," he said. "I can never be happy again if you leave. My father will not be coming. But he and I can serve you well, if we are permitted."

Sterekanda is awaited.

Jacob realized that the Cube was not answering him. He must try another way.

"Sterekanda will not leave Earth," he said.

Time passes. Within minutes it will be too late.

"Stay here," said Jacob. "Please, don't go."

Time has passed.

"I shall go to my father now," said Jacob, standing up and facing toward the door that must soon eject him. "Can I take a message to him?"

The door is sealed. Departure is imminent.

Even now, after such an explicit statement, Jacob did not appreciate the danger he was in. "Then I must go," he said.

The Cube was silent. The clock on the floor of the ship whirred and then sparked.

"What is happening?" said Jacob in sudden panic. "Let me go back to my father. Let me tell him whatever it is you want him to do."

The door is sealed.

"Unseal it," said Jacob, his voice rising. "I have to go back home."

Ormingat is home.

"Let me out!" shouted Jacob. "Ormingat is home, but not yet, and not without my father."

The door is sealed.

"Open it! Open it now and let me out!"

We do not have the technology.

"What do you mean?"

The door is sealed. The spaceship is on the point of departure.

Jacob flung himself at the place where the door should have been, but that was guesswork. There was now no evidence of any door at all. The ship was plunged into near darkness—even the Cube blanked out. In the base of the ship, on the laboratory side, the clock appeared huge, its stars and its wand the only visible light against black velvet.

Jacob stood gazing down at it, shocked into silence. He now understood completely that there was no going back. He could not even make any further appeal to the Cube, because it was no longer visible. All he could see was the clock, the wand a runnel full of stars.

He went on standing there, feeling chilled in the darkness, unable to think. Tears rolled down his cheeks, although he was not sobbing. He was not even fully aware of being sad. For more than an hour, he remained as still as a statue with no idea what he should do. He was afraid, deeply afraid, but it became a waiting fear, without direction.

Then suddenly there was motion; an upward thrust sent Jacob reeling back onto the sofa, where he huddled in terror. "I want my mother," he cried. "I want my mother."

It took an hour of Earth time for the takeoff to settle. Then the lights in the ship came back on, the ship's internal gravity asserted itself, and the Cube glowed green again.

You are traveling into space, Javayl ban. Have no fear.

The fox was no more than a meter away when the soil was scattered and the spaceship broke out from its prison and was flung miles up into the air, leaving briefly behind it a streak of blue light. The animal crouched down and whimpered, his ears sharp points against the side of his head. His fear was short-lived. Within less than a minute, he had recovered enough for curiosity to take him to the edge of the small hole the ship had made. He sniffed anxiously, scrabbled with his front paws, gulped down an earthworm, then sensibly gave up on the whole business and went on with his hunting.

CHAPTER 41

So Much to Tell

Steven did not sleep. He did not even nod. His eyes were on the screen, waiting for the moment of departure. Though what that would tell him goodness knows. He tried to see inside the ship, but that power was gone. All his abilities seemed to be diminishing. The picture on the screen was what the Brick chose to show him. No amount of manipulation would change the image.

The graveyard was barely discernible. The sky above it was dark with a hint of orange at its horizons from the streetlamps and the distant lights of London. Steven tried from time to time to change the image, to home in on the railings, to redirect the viewer. But it was of no avail. The machine was well and truly locked.

At two o'clock precisely, he saw exactly what he had been looking for: a spark of light came out of the grave like a soul ascending and whizzed off into the sky.

Now, surely now, the Brick would communicate. There must be things to tell.

The screen went blank.

It stayed blank for thirty minutes.

Steven pushed the lever and tried speaking to it again. "What is happening? I need to know what is happening!"

Nothing.

"Who is inside the spaceship?"

Silence.

"What is my function now?"

YOU HAVE NO FUNCTION.

It was a relief to see words appear on the screen. Even words as icy as these. They were, after all, a real answer to his question. The subject was open to argument, or so it seemed.

"Everyone has a function. I am here and I am alive."

The reply to this remark was no reply at all. Within seconds, words appeared on the screen that hit him as if he had been struck a real and very heavy blow.

YOUR SON IS SAFE. WE SHALL CARE FOR HIM.

Steven sat back in his chair and felt shivers run from head to foot. What did this mean? He knew what it might mean, but what it might mean was impossible. Surely it was impossible?

He ran down the stairs to Jacob's room, flung open the door, and shut his eyes in a swift prayer that his son would be lying sound asleep in bed. He wasn't. The bedclothes were ruffled as after a nightmare. Gasping, Steven raced back up to the computer room.

"Where is my son?" he demanded of the Brick. "What do you know of him?"

JAVAYL IS SAFE WITH US. HE IS OUR MOST TREASURED TRAVELER.

"*In the spaceship?*" said Steven, his voice a harsh whisper.

JAVAYL TRAVELS TO ORMINGAT. THERE WILL HIS HOME BE.

"His home is here on Earth," said Steven angrily. "Return him to us at once."

WE DO NOT HAVE THE TECHNOLOGY.

"Return to me command of the system," said Steven. "I shall produce the technology."

TOO FAR AWAY. OUT OF RANGE.

Another thought came to Steven. "Did my son go with you from choice? Did he want to go?"

The Brick paused a long time, its screen not dead but simply pearl gray.

"Come on," said Steven. "I deserve an answer."

HE IS AN ACCIDENTAL TRAVELER. THE DOORS SEALED AND COULD NOT BE OPENED. NO CRUELTY IS MEANT. IF WE KNEW HOW TO RETURN HIM TO YOU, WE WOULD.

"What am I to tell Lydia?" said Steven, looking down desperately at his own hands. "What am I to tell her?"

The screen cleared and in a short while another message scrolled into view.

YOUR SON HAS ABSCONDED. YOU KNOW NOT WHERE. THAT IS ALL THE EARTHLING NEEDS TO KNOW. THAT IS ALL SHE MUST EVER BE TOLD. BE LOYAL TO ORMINGAT IN THIS IF NOTHING ELSE.

Angrily, Steven rammed the screen down into the base behind the Brick. "I was talking to myself, object, not to you," he said harshly. "If I am no longer Ormingatrig, I am no longer subject to your commands."

To say that he never had been subject to anyone's commands would, at this point, be less than kind. The poor man was at his wits' end. His troubles were manifold. He had lost his son. He would have, somehow, to help his wife through this loss. And, suddenly feeling close to Matthew, he was also aware of having lost his own special place in the universe. Even if he managed to become fully committed to Earth, he would only ever be Earthling by adoption.

I have made a mess of everything, he thought. *Entesh, Argule. I do not know how to cope with this.*

Eventually, after sitting slumped in his chair for at least another two hours, he got up and resolutely left the room without a further glance toward the Brick.

I shall tell Lydia everything.

On his way downstairs Steven looked once more into Jacob's room, hoping against hope to find his son safe in his own bed. This time his gaze wandered from the empty bed to the rest of the room.

Jacob's clothes of the day before were neatly folded on the usual chair. His trainers were on the floor beside them. Hanging on the inside of the door was his dressing gown. So what was he wearing? A full change of clothing? A different pair of shoes?

Steven pulled back the sheets and lifted the pillow.

His pajamas aren't here.

Has he gone out into the night wearing only his pajamas?

He sat down on the side of Jacob's bed, gripping the mattress with each hand as if trying desperately to find something to hold on to.

It's no use. I shall tell Lydia everything. We'll have to work it out together.

He slipped into the room where she was still sleeping.

"Lydia," he said in a loud whisper. "Wake up, Lydia. There are things we need to talk about. Terrible things, and—oh, I am so sorry!"

Lydia sat up and swept her hair out of her eyes. She yawned as she made the effort to shake off sleep. "What is it?" she said. "What time is it? It can't be morning already."

"No, my love," said Steven, taking her hand gently in his. "It is not five o'clock yet. But you must wake up and listen. I have so much to tell you and I hardly know how to begin."

CHAPTER 42

The Cube

Jacob fell into a deep sleep from which he did not awake for several days. Ormingat knew how to cope with his pain and his terror. This was also the first stage of his conversion. Over the next three years, he would become Ormingatrig, body and mind, though his soul would remain unchanged and unchangeable, as all souls are.

When enough time had elapsed, he stirred and stretched and came awake on the sofa. The first thing he saw was the Cube, tilted as if it were looking down at him.

I am artifact, nonsentient being.

Jacob looked up fuzzily, heard the words, but did not quite believe them. In this terrible situation, still half-asleep, it seemed to him that the Cube was his only hope.

"Help me," he said. "I want to go home."

Sentient beings have programmed me to help you. I am to give you all you need, even love. For this journey I am your mother and father, your teacher and your friend. Call me Camballash.

Jacob was fully awake now, and the words of the Cube seemed filled with the assumption that all ties with Earth could be readily broken. A boy can sleep curled up like a baby, but in waking time he is nearer to being a man.

"I am fourteen years old," he said angrily, standing up and squaring his shoulders. "I am not a child to give a name to a doll."

The Cube ceased to tilt and its color faded to the palest green. *I am not a doll.*

"Turn this ship round and take me home," said Jacob in as commanding a voice as he could manage. His whole body trembled as he spoke, but the words came out firm and clear. He knew almost for certain what the answer would be, but he was determined to make the Cube understand that its offer of friendship was no solution. A speaking cube was a poor replacement for his mother, his father, and his sisters. *Give me all I need? Give me love? Who do you think you are?*

The Cube tilted once more and its voice when it spoke seemed to convey emotion. *We have not the technology. For you were the wrong time and place. We would never willingly have given unhappiness. If were the possibility, we would return you.*

In its errors, the nonsentient artifact sounded distressed. Was the distress built in? Was it part of the program?

Jacob sat down again and, resting his elbows on his knees, held his head between his hands. He felt guilty at having got himself into this situation. He thought of his mother, with all her quirky ways and fear of the outside world. It was so wrong to give her cause to weep. His father was more of a puzzle. Might he be glad that the ship was not returning empty? What would his sisters think about his disappearance? What would they be told?

The one thing he did not feel was fear for his own survival. The Cube gave him that reassurance at least. This was a journey and it would end, and at the end of it he would still be alive.

Accept, Javayl ban. There is no use to refuse. I am your friend. I am Camballash. I am to give, not to take. We cannot turn back, but forward is good.

Jacob looked up. He had gone over the edge of fear. The trembling suddenly left him and he knew the calmness of despair. There was no way out. If his heart should break, if he should beat the walls with his fists, or jump high enough to smash the

Cube, it would make no difference. The sleeping days had toughened him and he was fast learning how to cope, since cope he must.

He looked round the ship, appraising it as living quarters. His father had told him that the journey from Ormingat to Earth took three years. There was no reason to think that the return journey would be any shorter. Three years in solitary confinement, flying through space, was in itself a difficult idea to handle. How would it be managed? On a purely practical level it seemed impossible. What about food and drink? And what about the bathroom? He was suddenly aware that he was still dressed in pajamas. As if in answer to these thoughts, the Cube spoke again.

All is here for your requirements. Doors open. Cupboards have clothes. There is kitchen and bathroom as on Earth behind doors. There is all you need, Javayl.

Jacob looked behind him at the curved wall of the Earth "room" where he was sitting. Where the doors were was not clear. He was sufficiently interested to stand up and investigate further. That helped. As he walked toward the wall, a door slid open and within the recess he saw a bedroom very much like his own. As he turned to his left, the first door closed and another door opened to reveal a kitchen. Already he had enough of his new being working inside him to appreciate that this, though practical, was probably governed by illusion.

Accept everything. Questions can come later. This works.

"For now," said Jacob.

He spent hours after this exploring the possibilities of his new accommodation. He had a shower. He changed into day clothes— just a normal sweatshirt and jeans. Everything was there and everything fitted. He helped himself to cheese from the fridge and biscuits from the barrel. Then he made a pot of coffee.

"This is a sort of dream," he said to the Cube, "isn't it?"

The Cube did not answer.

"This coffee won't last three years," he said, smiling as his father would have done. "So it has to be dream coffee, or else I'll run out long before we get there."

Accept everything. Questions can come later. This works.

Now that Jacob had taken charge of himself, he felt in some way that he had also taken charge of the spaceship. The words of the Cube became clearer. He remembered his father's irritation when Jacob had called the Cube "friendly." But now, if ever, was the time for anthropomorphism.

"Very well," said Jacob. "Be my friend. I'll call you Cam. That other name you gave me is a bit of a mouthful."

Accepted. I am to be known as Cam.

Jacob sat back on the sofa and took stock of his situation. *I am not asleep. This is not a dream. But it is somehow a different sort of reality.*

Sleep again. In sleep you draw nearer to what you should be. In sleep you shall learn.

Jacob yawned. "Shall I go to bed?" he said. "Or shall I sleep here?"

The Cube did not reply.

"Cam," said Jacob. "Where shall I sleep?"

Choose, Javayl ban. The choice is yours.

"Do my parents know where I am?" said Jacob sleepily. "They must be worried about me. Surely my father could use the Brick to get me back."

There was no answer. Cam had not heard of the Brick. This name for the protection module was not in the program. The communicator was not equipped to ask for clarification.

As Jacob stretched out on the sofa, he knew that this was no more than a token protest, a dutiful idea. Already he was accepting, as Cam had told him to accept. His soul would always be his own, wherever he might find himself, but his mind and body were changing. And the change felt good.

CHAPTER 43

The Brick

Steven's revelations left Lydia stunned. He had told her absolutely everything. Together they checked Jacob's room, ransacked it almost, and came to the conclusion that he must indeed have gone out clad only in his pajamas.

"He could be sleepwalking," said Lydia. "We should go out and look for him."

"We know he is not sleepwalking," said Steven gently. "Neither is he lost. He is in a spaceship traveling out of this solar system into another. We know that."

"*You* know that," said Lydia, but her protest had no strength in it.

"*We* know that," said Steven.

She could not contradict him.

The story Steven had just told her had begun with the motivil and how it had saved Jacob's life. There had been something very decisive about that. It now seemed to her that her son had been hers "on loan." It was as if the earthly Jacob had died all those years ago, and she had been given some sort of changeling. *He is not flesh of my flesh.* Yet nothing in the whole of creation could alter the fact that she was his mother and had reared him from babyhood.

They went silently down to the sitting room, where they sat

together on the settee. The room was in semidarkness, lit only by the table lamp. Upstairs, the twins would be sleeping.

"I want to see the Brick," said Lydia. "I do believe you—why would you want to lie to me?—but I must see the Brick at work."

"I don't know if it will work for you—I mean, in your presence. It can be temperamental at the best of times," said Steven doubtfully. He was reluctant to make the attempt. He was not sure whether the protection module would know that there was an illegal observer watching the screen.

"I won't speak," said Lydia, knowing the thoughts her husband had not put into words. "I'll sneak in quietly and won't even move till you have done all that needs to be done."

They walked furtively up the two flights of stairs, trying their best to let no stair creak. It was important not to wake the twins.

Steven opened the door to the computer room and sat Lydia down in the armchair, turning it very carefully so that it would face the screen. The only light would be the lamp on the desk, so she would be hidden in shadow.

He sat down in front of the Brick, unscrolled the screen, pressed the buttons to give him a visual image, and waited. At first the screen was entirely blank and he half expected to see no more than a farewell message, if that.

Then suddenly, there was a picture of the inside of the spaceship. All was still. On the sofa, Jacob was lying curled up and fast asleep.

Lydia craned forward and gasped involuntarily. Steven turned toward her for a second, no more, and put one finger to his lips. When he turned back, the screen was blank again. Fiercely he pulled the lever that would allow him to speak to the module.

"What happened to the picture?" he said. "I want to see my son."

OUT OF RANGE.

"What do you mean?" said Steven. "We have just seen him."

"You have seen him," said Steven rapidly. "I have seen him. You and I are *we*."

Lydia shrank back into the cushions of the armchair, realizing that it was very important that the machine should be totally unaware of her presence.

OUT OF RANGE NOW. NO MORE WE CAN SEE HIM.

"Is he really safe? Will he be happy?" said Steven. These questions were specifically to elicit an answer for Lydia.

JAVAYL IS SAFER THAN ON EARTH. HE WILL BE HAPPIER THAN HE EVER WAS IN HIS LONELY LIFE ON THAT PLANET.

Steven unscrolled the screen and switched the protection module to its rest position. Now it was safe for him to speak to Lydia. He turned on the light to check the room before leaving.

"I'll try again later," he said feebly, knowing that later would be worse rather than better. Out of range now would be well and truly out of range later.

Lydia gave him a wan smile. There were so many things she knew without being told.

"We could be given more information," said Steven, understanding her cynicism. "They might still want me to work for them."

He opened the door and turned to switch off the light. He and Lydia together looked across at the Brick. What they saw told them all they would ever know.

On the shelf, where the Brick had been, was an ordinary builder's brick, orange and porous, with not a button in sight.

Steven dashed over to it, searched behind it for the screen and its frame. There was nothing there.

LAMBERT BRICK CO. were the words embossed within the brick's borders. Steven picked it up in his hands, turned it round and round, and was about to fling it to the floor when he remembered the sleepers in the room below. Lydia took it from him and put it back on the table.

"You know now," said Steven. "You know all there is to know."

"I know," said Lydia. "I do know now. But that does not make it any less terrible."

Steven grasped her arm in an attempt to comfort. "We won't be alone," he said. "My people are not cruel and, though they lack the ability to return our son to us, there are other ways in which they will help."

Lydia was puzzled. "We'll see them?" she said. "I don't follow."

"We'll not see them or know them, but they will do everything to protect us and to ease the pain. The Brick was a protection module. There are other protection modules. I know we will not be left entirely alone," said Steven.

They returned to the sitting room and, for some time, sat in silence.

"I used to think it was my fault," said Lydia. The skin seemed stretched tight across her face and her lips were bloodless.

"What was your fault?" said Steven, not sure what this remark might mean.

"I used to think it was from me that Jacob inherited his loneliness," she said. "You called me a waif-soul. I thought my son was just such another, and that the fault was mine."

"Life's not as simple as that," said Steven. "That is an Earth way of looking at things—heredity, environment. They are valid up to a point, but every soul in the universe—and God alone knows how many or how scattered they might be—is an individual. We are not peas in a pod."

Then Lydia thought of Jacob, her own very individual son, and for the first time since all this was sprung upon her, she began to weep and weep as if she would never stop.

Steven put his arms around her and he too sobbed quietly.

Where was Ormingat protection from such sorrow?

There is an answer: sometimes the only thing left to do is to weep.

"He's not dead, you know," said Steven at last, in a voice hoarse with emotion. "And he will be happy. Just think that he has grown up a little faster. It is as if he had emigrated."

True comfort came much, much later.

To Lydia was vouchsafed one brief, bright vision of Jacob's arrival on a planet far away. She lit just one candle on her son's seventeenth birthday. She watched it burn, and in its flame she saw the joy of Ormingat.

The Faraway Planet

Javayl was suddenly aware of a change in the motion of the spaceship. In the past three years he had become accustomed to the quiet buzz of its engines, a buzz very near to silence but suggesting great speed. Now the buzz was more perceptible and there had been a sharp jolt in the ship's movement.

"*What is it?*" he said, looking up at the Cube. "*Is there a fault somewhere, Cam?*"

He was now speaking in the voice and the language of Ormingat, though he was not yet aware of the change: others would have to explain it to him later.

We are arriving in Ormingat. The ship has slowed down. Everything is going as planned. Have no fear, Javayl ban.

The voice of the communicator still sounded tinny, but its speech was clear and correct. The language of Ormingat was easier to transmit. Translation was no longer needed.

Lie down and close your eyes. That is best.

Javayl did as he was told. The Earth-simulated side of the ship was the same as it had always been, but now it seemed alien, like something that might feature in a science museum. For more than a year now, Javayl had felt like a visitor there, just waiting to get to his real home.

The ship glided into the atmosphere of Ormingat.

Javayl felt it bounce lightly as if landing on an enormous feather pillow, though now the Earth simile would be lost on him. He was Ormingatrig to the core. When the motion stopped entirely, he opened his eyes and the room that had been his for three whole years had disappeared. What he saw, where he was, he instantly understood. This was Ormingat living space, indescribable on Earth, but full of comfort and beauty.

It is time to leave me now. Goodbye, Javayl ban.

The communicator sounded regretful, but that, of course, was impossible. Machines have no regrets.

Javayl lifted one hand in farewell to the Cube. *"I shall not forget you, Cam. You have been a good friend to me."*

Then he went to what he knew to be the doorway. It opened outward and downward. The first surprise Javayl had was to see that the spaceship was no smaller outside than in. It was a full-sized spaceship resting on a circular pad that had clearly been prepared for its arrival.

Javayl stepped down the ramp and onto Ormingat. The door folded up into the side of the spaceship, locking the Cube inside. Now Javayl was alone on a strange planet.

Yet it did not feel strange, or look strange, or smell strange. All around him were features that made more sense to him than anything on Earth could ever do now.

"Welcome," said a voice behind him in the beautiful, musical tongue of Ormingat. No screeching now, just the right voice in the right place. To hear it gave Javayl a feeling of warmth as if the sound were embracing him, but he did not turn round to face the speaker.

He looked ahead of him and saw that he was on the shore of a silver lake, in whose rippling water were reflected two suns, one close and large and bright, one much further off and smaller.

He stepped down toward the lake and looked at his reflection. His appearance was totally different from that of Jacob on Earth. Yet he recognized himself immediately. *That is myself. That is what I look like.*

"*We have waited so long for you*," said another voice behind him, too far away for its owner to be reflected in the water.

Javayl still did not look round. Instead he gazed across the wide lake to a distant shore, seeing much that cannot be expressed in human terms. The space above him seemed more closely related to infinity, and all around was the beauty that is truth. Everything there, above and beneath him, before and behind him, from the greatest to the least, seemed to say, *This is myself. . . . This is what I truly look like. . . . Learn me and love me.*

"I am Tonitheen," said another voice, gently breaking in on his thoughts. "*We can be friends. Friendship is as important here on Ormingat as it is on Earth.*"

Still Javayl did not look round. He was aware of more and more movement, as if a whole company were gathering, but he was not ready for them yet. There was something important he still needed to know. Not even Tonitheen's offer of friendship could take this burden from him. Who was Tonitheen anyway? Javayl had lost his memory of most of the things that had made up his life on Earth. His Ormingat brain was filling with other, different information. The name Tonitheen was vaguely familiar, its connotation vaguely pleasant. That was all.

"*There is something I have to know,*" he said, addressing the sky and the shimmering lake, anything but the voices behind him.

"Ask," said a different, older voice. It sounded womanly. On Ormingat clearly there were male and female as on Earth. "*All you have to do is ask.*"

"*Who am I?*" said Javayl in a voice no higher than a whisper. "*Who truly knows me?*"

"I know you," said the woman, her voice ringing out like a bell. "I *would know you anywhere. You are my grandson, son of my beloved Sterekanda. Come to me, Javayl ban.*"

Then the young man who was Javayl turned round and saw a host of faces all smiling at him, all delighted to see him. *We know you, we need you, and we love you. . . .*

In their midst Javayl recognized his grandmother, whom he was seeing for the first time, but that is not how it seemed to him. He ran to her side, instantly finding in her the family he had lost.

"*Welcome, Javayl ban,*" she said softly. "*Welcome home.*"

And all around them, the Ormingatrig joined in.

"*Welcome to Ormingat, Javayl berenishta.*"

About the Author

Sylvia Waugh is the author of *Space Race* (a companion to *Earthborn* and *Who Goes Home?*), which was an ALA Notable Book, a *Horn Book* Fanfare, and a *School Library Journal* Best Book of the Year.

Sylvia Waugh's first book, *The Mennyms*, was published in England in 1993 and was an immediate success with reviewers and teachers. It won the *Guardian* Children's Fiction Prize and was short-listed for Great Britain's highest literary award, the Carnegie Medal. Her other books include *Mennyms into the Wilderness* and *Mennyms Alive*.

A retired teacher, Sylvia Waugh lives in the North of England with her three grown-up children.